Freeman Wills Crofts w
died in 1957. He worked
company as an engineer, v
he moved to England and t
full-time.

His plots reveal his mathematical training and he specialised in the seemingly unbreakable alibi and the intricacies of railway timetables. He also loved ships and trains and they feature in many of his stories.

Crofts' best-known character is Inspector Joseph French, a detective who achieves his results through dogged persistence.

Raymond Chandler praised Crofts' plots, calling him 'the soundest builder of them all'.

BY THE SAME AUTHOR
ALL PUBLISHED BY HOUSE OF STRATUS

FREEMAN WILLS CROFTS

The Mystery of the
Sleeping Car Express
and other stories

HOUSE OF
STRATUS

This edition published in 2001 by House of Stratus, an imprint of
House of Stratus Ltd, Thirsk Industrial Park, York Road, Thirsk,
North Yorkshire, YO7 3BX, UK.
Also at: House of Stratus Inc., 2 Neptune Road, Poughkeepsie, NY 12601, USA.

www.houseofstratus.com

Typeset by House of Stratus, printed and bound by Short Run Press Limited.

A catalogue record for this book is available from the British Library
and the Library of Congress.

ISBN 1-84232-407-1

In this collection of stories Inspector French, Freeman Wills Crofts' legendary detective, once again shows his mettle. The volume is really a series of mental exercises for the reader. In each case the murderer gives the game away to the investigator. Can the reader spot this before Inspector French explains it?

CONTENTS

THE MYSTERY OF
THE SLEEPING CAR EXPRESS

No one who was in England in the autumn of 1909 can fail
to remember the terrible tragedy which took place in a
North-Western express between Preston and Carlisle. The
affair attracted enormous attention at the time, not only
because of the arresting nature of the events themselves,
but even more for the absolute mystery in which they were
shrouded.

Quite lately a singular chance has revealed to me the true
explanation of this terrible drama, and it is at the express
desire of its chief actor that I now take upon myself to make
the facts known. As it is a long time since 1909, I may,
perhaps, be pardoned if I first recall the events which came
to light at the time.

One Thursday, then, early in November of the year in
question, the 10.30 p.m. sleeping car train left Euston as
usual for Edinburgh, Glasgow, and the North. It was
generally a heavy train, being popular with businessmen
who liked to complete their day's work in London, sleep
while travelling, and arrive at their northern destination
with time for a leisurely bath and breakfast before office
hours. The night in question was no exception to the rule,
and two engines hauled behind them eight large sleeping
cars, two firsts, two thirds, and two vans, half of which went
to Glasgow, and the remainder to Edinburgh.

It is essential to the understanding of what follows that the composition of the rear portion of the train should be remembered. At the extreme end came the Glasgow van, a long eight-wheeled, bogie vehicle, with Guard Jones in charge. Next to the van was one of the third-class coaches, in front of it a first-class, and then one of the sleeping cars, all labelled for the same city. These coaches were fairly well filled, particularly the third-class. The train was corridor throughout, and the officials could, and did, pass through it several times during the journey.

It is with the first-class coach that we are principally concerned, and it will be understood from the above that it was placed in between the sleeping car in front and the third-class behind, the van following immediately behind the third. It had a lavatory at each end and six compartments, the last two, next the third-class, being smokers, the next three non-smoking, and the first, immediately beside the sleeping car, a 'Ladies Only'. The corridors in both it and the third-class coach were on the left-hand side in the direction of travel – that is, the compartments were on the side of the double line.

The night was dark as the train drew out of Euston, for there was no moon and the sky was overcast. As was remembered and commented on afterwards, there had been an unusually long spell of dry weather, and, though it looked like rain earlier in the evening, none fell till the next day, when, about six in the morning, there was a torrential downpour.

As the detectives pointed out later, no weather could have been more unfortunate from their point of view, as, had footmarks been made during the night, the ground would have been too hard to take good impressions, while even such traces as remained would more than likely have been blurred by the rain.

The train ran to time, stopping at Rugby, Crewe and Preston. After leaving the latter station Guard Jones found he had occasion to go forward to speak to a ticket collector in the Edinburgh portion. He accordingly left his van in the rear and passed along the corridor of the third-class carriage adjoining.

At the end of this corridor, beside the vestibule joining it to the first-class, were a lady and gentleman, evidently husband and wife, the lady endeavouring to soothe the cries of a baby she was carrying. Guard Jones addressed some civil remark to the man, who explained that their child had been taken ill, and they had brought it out of their compartment as it was disturbing the other passengers.

With an expression of sympathy, Jones unlocked the two doors across the corridor at the vestibule between the carriages, and, passing on into the first-class coach, reclosed them behind him. They were fitted with spring locks, which became fast on the door shutting.

The corridor of the first-class coach was empty, and as Jones walked down it he observed that the blinds of all the compartments were lowered, with one exception – that of the 'Ladies Only'. In this compartment, which contained three ladies, the light was fully on, and the guard noticed that two out of the three were reading.

Continuing his journey, Jones found that the two doors at the vestibule between the first-class coach and the sleeper were also locked, and he opened them and passed through, shutting them behind him. At the sleeping car attendant's box, just inside the last of these doors, two car attendants were talking together. One was actually inside the box, the other standing in the corridor. The latter moved aside to let the guard pass, taking up his former position as, after exchanging a few words, Jones moved on.

His business with the ticket collector finished, Guard Jones returned to his van. On this journey he found the same conditions obtaining as on the previous – the two attendants were at the rear end of the sleeping car, the lady and gentleman with the baby in the front end of the third-class coach, the first-class corridor deserted, and both doors at each end of the latter coach locked. These details, casually remarked at the time, became afterwards of the utmost importance, adding as they did to the mystery in which the tragedy was enveloped.

About an hour before the train was due at Carlisle, while it was passing through the wild moorland country of the Westmorland highlands, the brakes were applied – at first gently, and then with considerable power. Guard Jones, who was examining parcel waybills in the rear end of his van, supposed it to be a signal check, but as such was unusual at this place, he left his work and walking down the van, lowered the window at the left-hand side and looked out along the train.

The line happened to be in a cutting, and the railway bank for some distance ahead was dimly illuminated by the light from the corridors of the first and third-class coaches immediately in front of his van. As I have said, the night was dark, and, except for this bit of bank, Jones could see nothing ahead. The railway curved away to the right, so, thinking he might see better from the other side, he crossed the van and looked out of the opposite window, next to the up line.

There were no signal lights in view, nor anything to suggest the cause of the slack, but as he ran his eye along the train, he saw that something was amiss in the first-class coach. From the window at its rear end figures were leaning, gesticulating wildly, as if to attract attention to some grave and pressing danger. The guard at once ran through the third-class to this coach, and there he found a strange and puzzling state of affairs.

The corridor was still empty, but the centre blind of the rear compartment – that is, the first reached by the guard – had been raised. Through the glass Jones could see that the compartment contained four men. Two were leaning out of the window on the opposite side, and two were fumbling at the latch of the corridor door, as if trying to open it. Jones caught hold of the outside handle to assist, but they pointed in the direction of the adjoining compartment, and the guard, obeying their signs, moved on to the second door.

The centre blind of this compartment had also been pulled up, though here, again, the door had not been opened. As the guard peered in through the glass he saw that he was in the presence of tragedy.

Tugging desperately at the handle of the corridor door stood a lady, her face blanched, her eyes, starting from her head, her features frozen into an expression of deadly fear and horror. As she pulled she kept glancing over her shoulder, as if some dreadful apparition lurked in the shadows behind. As Jones sprang forward to open the door his eyes followed the direction of her gaze, and he drew in his breath sharply.

At the far side of the compartment, facing the engine and huddled down in the corner, was the body of a woman. She lay limp and inert, with head tilted back at an unnatural angle into the cushions and a hand hanging helplessly down over the edge of the seat. She might have been thirty years of age, and was dressed in a reddish-brown fur coat with toque to match. But these details the guard hardly

5

glanced at, his attention being riveted to her forehead. There, above the left eyebrow, was a sinister little hole, from which the blood had oozed down the coat and formed a tiny pool on the seat. That she was dead was obvious.

But this was not all. On the seat opposite her lay a man, and, as far as Guard Jones could see, he also was dead.

He apparently had been sitting in the corner seat, and had fallen forward so that his chest lay across the knees of the woman and his head hung down towards the floor. He was all bunched and twisted up – just a shapeless mass in a grey frieze overcoat, with dark hair at the back of what could be seen of his head. But under that head the guard caught the glint of falling drops, while a dark, ominous stain grew on the floor beneath.

Jones flung himself on the door, but it would not move. It stood fixed, an inch open, jammed in some mysterious way, imprisoning the lady with her terrible companions.

As she and the guard strove to force it open, the train came to a standstill. At once it occurred to Jones that he could now enter the compartment from the opposite side.

Shouting to reassure the now almost frantic lady, he turned back to the end compartment, intending to pass through it on to the line and so back to that containing the bodies. But here he was again baffled, for the two men had not succeeded in sliding back their door. He seized the handle to help them, and then he noticed their companions had opened the opposite door and were climbing out on to the permanent way.

It flashed through his mind that an up-train passed about this time, and, fearing an accident, he ran down the corridor to the sleeping car, where he felt sure he would find a door that would open. That at the near end was free, and he leaped out on to the track. As he passed he shouted to one of the attendants to follow him, and to the other to remain where he was and let no one pass. Then he joined the men who had already alighted, warned them about the up-train, and the four opened the outside door of the compartment in which the tragedy had taken place.

Their first concern was to get the uninjured lady out, and here a difficult and ghastly task awaited them. The door was blocked by the bodies, and its narrowness prevented more than one man, from working. Sending the car attendant to search the train for a doctor, Jones clambered up, and, after warning the lady not to look at what he was doing, he raised the man's body and propped it back in the corner seat.

The face was a strong one with clean-shaven but rather coarse features, a large nose, and a heavy jaw. In the neck, just below the right ear, was a bullet hole which, owing to the position of the head, had bled freely. As far as the guard could see, the man was dead. Not without a certain shrinking, Jones raised the feet, first of the man, and then of the woman, and placed them on the seats, thus leaving the floor clear except for its dark, creeping pool. Then,

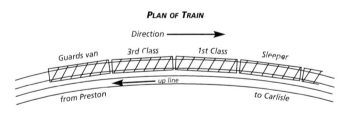

PLAN OF TRAIN

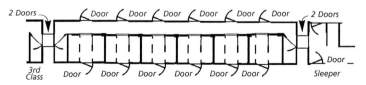

ENLARGEMENT OF FIRST CLASS COACH

placing his handkerchief over the dead woman's face, he rolled back the end of the carpet to hide its sinister stain.

'Now, ma'am, if you please,' he said; and keeping the lady with her back to the more gruesome object on the opposite seat, he helped her to the open door, from where willing hands assisted her to the ground.

By this time, the attendant had found a doctor in the third-class coach, and a brief examination enabled him to pronounce both victims dead. The blinds in the compartment having been drawn down and the outside door locked, the guard called to those passengers who had alighted to resume their seats, with a view to continuing their journey.

The fireman had meantime come back along the train to ascertain what was wrong, and to say the driver was unable completely to release the brake. An examination was therefore made, and the tell-tale disc at the end of the first-class coach was found to be turned, showing that someone in that carriage had pulled the communication chain. This, as is perhaps not generally known, allows air to pass between the train pipe and the atmosphere, thereby gently applying the brake and preventing its complete release. Further investigation showed that the slack of the chain was hanging in the end smoking-compartment, indicating that the alarm must have been operated by one of the four men who travelled there. The disc was then turned back to normal, the passengers reseated, and the train started, after a delay of about fifteen minutes.

Before reaching Carlisle, Guard Jones took the name and address of everyone travelling in the first and third-class coaches, together with the numbers of their tickets. These coaches, as well as the van, were thoroughly searched, and it was established beyond any doubt that no one was concealed under the seats, in the lavatories, behind luggage, or, in fact, anywhere about them.

One of the sleeping car attendants having been in the corridor in the rear of the last sleeper from the Preston stop till the completion of this search, and being positive no one except the guard had passed during that time, it was not considered necessary to take the names of the passengers in the sleeping cars, but the numbers of their tickets were noted.

On arrival at Carlisle the matter was put into the hands of the police. The first-class carriage was shunted off, the doors being locked and sealed, and the passengers who had travelled in it were detained to make their statements. Then began a most careful and searching investigation, as a result of which several additional facts became known.

The first step taken by the authorities was to make an examination of the country surrounding the point at which the train had stopped, in the hope of finding traces of some stranger on the line. The tentative theory was that a murder had been committed and that the murderer had escaped from the train when it stopped, struck across the country, and, gaining some road, had made good his escape.

Accordingly, as soon as it was light, a special train brought a force of detectives to the place, and the railway, as well as a tract of ground on each side of it, was subjected to a prolonged and exhaustive search. But no traces were found. Nothing that a stranger might have dropped was picked up, no footsteps were seen, no marks discovered. As has already been stated, the weather was against the searchers. The drought of the previous days had left the ground hard and unyielding, so that clear impressions were scarcely to be expected, while even such as might have been made were not likely to remain after the downpour of the early morning.

Baffled at this point, the detectives turned their attention to the stations in the vicinity. There were only two within walking distance of the point of the tragedy, and at neither had any stranger been seen. Further, no trains had stopped at either of these stations; indeed, not a single train, either passenger or goods, had stopped anywhere in the neighbourhood since the sleeping car express went through. If the murderer had left the express, it was, therefore, out of the question that he could have escaped by rail.

The investigators then turned their attention to the country roads and adjoining towns, trying to find the trail – if there was a trail – while it was hot. But here, again, no luck attended their efforts. If there were a murderer, and if he had left the train when it stopped, he had vanished into thin air. No traces of him could anywhere be discovered.

Nor were their researches in other directions much more fruitful.

The dead couple were identified as a Mr and Mrs Horatio Llewelyn, of Gordon Villa, Broad Road, Halifax. Mr Llewelyn was the junior partner of a large firm of Yorkshire ironfounders. A man of five-and-thirty, he moved in good society and had some claim to wealth. He was of kindly though somewhat passionate disposition, and, so far as could be learnt, had not an enemy in the world. His firm was able to show that he had had business appointments in London on the Thursday and in Carlisle on the Friday, so that his travelling by the train in question was quite in accordance with his known plans.

His wife was the daughter of a neighbouring merchant, a pretty girl of some seven-and-twenty. They had been married only a little over a month, and had, in fact, only a week earlier returned from their honeymoon. Whether Mrs Llewelyn had any definite reason for accompanying her husband on the fatal journey could not be ascertained. She also, so far as was known, had no enemy, nor could any motive for the tragedy be suggested.

The extraction of the bullets proved that the same weapon had been used in each case – a revolver of small bore and modern design. But as many thousands of similar revolvers existed, this discovery led to nothing.

Miss Blair-Booth, the lady who had travelled with the Llewelyns, stated she had joined the train at Euston, and occupied one of the seats next to the corridor. A couple of minutes before starting the deceased had arrived, and they sat in the two opposite corners. No other passengers had entered the compartment during the journey, nor had any of the three left it; in fact, except for the single visit of the ticket collector shortly after leaving Euston, the door into the corridor had not been even opened.

Mr Llewelyn was very attentive to his young wife, and they had conversed for some time after starting, then, after consulting Miss Blair-Booth, he had pulled down the blinds and shaded the light, and they had settled down for the night. Miss Blair-Booth had slept at intervals, but each time she wakened she had looked round the compartment, and everything was as before. Then she was suddenly aroused from a doze by a loud explosion close by.

She sprang up, and as she did so a flash came from somewhere near her knee, and a second explosion sounded. Startled and trembling, she pulled the shade off the lamp, and then she noticed a little cloud of smoke just inside the corridor door, which had been opened about an inch, and smelled the characteristic odour of burnt powder. Swinging round, she was in time to see Mr Llewelyn dropping heavily forward across his wife's knees, and then she observed the mark on the latter's forehead and realized they had both been shot.

Terrified, she raised the blind of the corridor door which covered the handle and tried to get out to call assistance. But she could not move the door, and her horror was not diminished when she found herself locked in with what she rightly believed were two dead bodies. In despair she pulled the communication chain, but the train did not appear to stop, and she continued struggling with the door till, after what seemed to her hours, the guard appeared, and she was eventually released.

In answer to a question, she further stated that when her blind went up the corridor was empty, and she saw no one till the guard came.

The four men in the end compartment were members of one party travelling from London to Glasgow. For some time after leaving they had played cards, but, about midnight, they, too, had pulled down their blinds, shaded the lamp, and composed themselves to sleep. In this case also, no person other than the ticket collector had entered the compartment during the journey. But after leaving Preston the door had been opened. Aroused by the stop, one of the men had eaten some fruit, and having thereby soiled his fingers, had washed them in the lavatory. The door then had opened as usual. This man saw no one in the corridor, nor did he notice anything out of the common.

Some time after this all four were startled by the sound of two shots. At first they thought of fog signals, then, realizing they were too far from the engine to hear such, they, like Miss Blair-Booth, unshaded their lamp, raised the blind over their corridor door, and endeavoured to leave the compartment. Like her they found themselves unable to open their door, and, like her also, they saw that there was no one in the corridor. Believing something serious had happened, they pulled the communication chain, at the same time lowering the outside window and waving from it in the hope of attracting attention. The chain came down easily as if slack, and this explained the apparent contradiction between Miss Blair-Booth's statement that she had pulled it; and the fact that the slack was found hanging in the end compartment. Evidently the lady had pulled it first, applying the brake and the second pull had simply transferred the slack from one compartment to the next.

The two compartments in front of that of the tragedy were found to be empty when the train stopped, but in the last of the non-smoking compartments were two gentlemen, and in the 'Ladies Only', three ladies. All these had heard the shots, but so faintly above the noise of the train that the attention of none of them was specially arrested, nor had they attempted any investigation. The gentlemen had not left their compartment or pulled up their blinds between the time the train left Preston and the emergency stop, and could throw no light whatever on the matter.

The three ladies in the end compartment were a mother and two daughters, and had got in at Preston. As they were alighting at Carlisle they had not wished to sleep, so they had left their blinds up and their light unshaded. Two of them were reading, but the third was seated at the corridor side, and this lady stated positively that no one except the guard had passed while they were in the train.

She described his movements – first, towards the engine, secondly, back towards the van, and a third time, running, towards the engine just before the train stopped – so accurately in accord with the other evidence that considerable reliance was placed on her testimony. The stoppage and the guard's haste had aroused her interest, and all three ladies had immediately come out into the corridor, and had remained there till the train proceeded, and all three were satisfied that no one else had passed during that time.

An examination of the doors which had jammed so mysteriously revealed the fact that a small wooden wedge, evidently designed for the purpose, had been driven in between the floor and the bottom of the framing of the door, holding the latter rigid. It was evident therefore that the crime was premeditated, and the details had been carefully worked out beforehand. The most careful search of the carriage failed to reveal any other suspicious object or mark.

On comparing the tickets issued with those held by the passengers, a discrepancy was discovered. All were accounted for except one. A first single for Glasgow had been issued at Euston for the train in question, which had not been collected. The purchaser had therefore either not travelled at all, or had got out at some intermediate station. In either case no demand for a refund had been made.

The collector who had checked the tickets after the train had left London believed, though he could not speak positively, that two men had then occupied the non-smoking compartment next to that in which the tragedy had occurred, one of whom held a Glasgow ticket, and the other a ticket for an intermediate station. He could not recollect which station nor could he describe either of the men, if indeed they were there at all.

But the ticket collector's recollection was not at fault, for the police succeeded in tracing one of the passengers, a Dr

Hill, who had got out at Crewe. He was able, partially at all events, to account for the missing Glasgow ticket. It appeared that when he joined the train at Euston, a man of about five-and-thirty was already in the compartment. This man had fair hair, blue eyes, and a full moustache, and was dressed in dark, well-cut clothes. He had no luggage, but only a waterproof and a paper-covered novel. The two travellers had got into conversation, and on the stranger learning that the doctor lived at Crewe, said he was alighting there also, and asked to be recommended to an hotel. He then explained that he had intended to go on to Glasgow and had taken a ticket to that city, but had since decided to break his journey to visit a friend in Chester next day. He asked the doctor if he thought his ticket would be available to complete the journey the following night, and if not, whether he could get a refund.

When they reached Crewe, both these travellers had alighted, and the doctor offered to show his acquaintance the entrance to the Crewe Arms, but the stranger, thanking him, declined, saying he wished to see to his luggage. Dr Hill saw him walking towards the van as he left the platform.

Upon interrogating the staff on duty at Crewe at the time, no one could recall seeing such a man at the van, nor had any inquiries about the luggage been made. But as these facts did not come to light until several days after the tragedy, confirmation was hardly to be expected.

A visit to all the hotels in Crewe and Chester revealed the fact that no one in any way resembling the stranger had stayed there, nor could any trace whatever be found of him.

Such were the principal facts made known at the adjourned inquest on the bodies of Mr and Mrs Llewelyn. It was confidently believed that a solution to the mystery would speedily be found, but as day after day passed away without bringing to light any fresh information, public interest began to wane, and became directed into other channels.

But for a time controversy over the affair waxed keen. At first it was argued that it was a case of suicide, some holding that Mr Llewelyn had shot first his wife and then himself; others that both had died by the wife's hand. But this theory had only to be stated to be disproved.

Several persons hastened to point out that not only had the revolver disappeared, but on neither body was there powder blackening, and it was admitted that such a wound could not be self-inflicted without leaving marks from this source. That murder had been committed was therefore clear.

Rebutted on this point, the theorists then argued that Miss Blair-Booth was the assassin. But here again the suggestion was quickly negatived. The absence of motive, her known character and the truth of such of her statements as could be checked were against the idea. The disappearance of the revolver was also in her favour. As it was not in the compartment nor concealed about her person, she could only have rid herself of it out of the window. But the position of the bodies prevented access to the window, and, as her clothes were free from any stain of blood, it was impossible to believe she had moved these grim relics, even had she been physically able.

But the point that finally demonstrated her innocence was the wedging of the corridor door. It was obvious she could not have wedged the door on the outside and then passed through it. The belief was universal that whoever wedged the door fired the shots, and the fact that the former was wedged an inch open strengthened that view, as the motive was clearly to leave a slot through which to shoot.

Lastly, the medical evidence showed that if the Llewelyns were sitting where Miss Blair-Booth stated, and the shots were fired from where she said, the bullets would have entered the bodies from the direction they were actually found to have done.

But Miss Blair-Booth's detractors were loath to recede from the position they had taken up. They stated that of the objections to their theory only one – the wedging of the doors – was overwhelming. And they advanced an ingenious theory to meet it. They suggested that before reaching Preston Miss Blair-Booth had left the compartment, closing the door after her, that she had then wedged it, and that, on stopping at the station, she had passed out through some other compartment, re-entering her own through the outside door.

In answer to this it was pointed out that the gentleman who had eaten the fruit had opened his door *after* the Preston stop, and if Miss Blair-Booth was then shut into her compartment she could not have wedged the other door. That two people should be concerned in the wedging was unthinkable. It was therefore clear that Miss Blair-Booth was innocent, and that some other person had wedged both doors, in order to prevent his operations in the corridor being interfered with by those who would hear the shots.

It was recognized that similar arguments applied to the four men in the end compartment – the wedging of the doors cleared them also.

Defeated on these points the theorists retired from the field. No further suggestions were put forward by the public or the daily Press. Even to those behind the scenes the case seemed to become more and more difficult the longer it was pondered.

Each person known to have been present came in turn under the microscopic eye of New Scotland Yard, but each in turn had to be eliminated from suspicion, till it almost seemed proved that no murder could have been committed at all. The prevailing mystification was well summed up by the Chief at the Yard in conversation with the Inspector in charge of the case.

'A troublesome business, certainly,' said the great man, 'and I admit that your conclusions seem sound. But let us go over it again. There *must* be a flaw somewhere.'

'There must, sir. But I've gone over it and over it till I'm stupid, and every time I get the same result.'

'We'll try once more. We begin, then, with a murderer in a railway carriage. We're sure it was a murder, of course?'

'Certainly, sir. The absence of the revolver and of powder blackening and the wedging of the doors prove it.'

'Quite. The murder must therefore have been committed by some person who was either in the carriage when it was searched, or had left before that. Let us take these two possibilities in turn. And first, with regard to the searching. Was that efficiently done?'

'Absolutely, sir. I have gone into it with the guard and attendants. No one could have been overlooked.'

'Very good. Taking first, then, those who were in the carriage. There were six compartments. In the first were the four men, and in the second, Miss Blair-Booth. Are you satisfied these were innocent?'

'Perfectly, sir. The wedging of the doors eliminated them.'

'So I think. The third and fourth compartments were empty, but in the fifth there were two gentlemen. What about them?'

'Well, sir, you know who they were. Sir Gordon M'Clean, the great engineer, and Mr Silas Hemphill, the professor of Aberdeen University. Both utterly beyond suspicion.'

'But, as you know, inspector, *no one* is beyond suspicion in a case of this kind.'

'I admit it, sir, and therefore I made careful inquiries about them. But I only confirmed my opinion.'

'From inquiries I also have made I feel sure you are right. That brings us to the last compartment, the "Ladies Only". What about those three ladies?'

'The same remarks apply. Their characters are also beyond suspicion, and, as well as that, the mother is elderly and timid, and couldn't brazen out a lie. I question if the daughters could either. I made inquiries all the same, and found not the slightest ground for suspicion.'

'The corridors and lavatories were empty?'

'Yes, sir.'

'Then everyone found in the coach when the train stopped may be definitely eliminated?'

'Yes. It is quite impossible it could have been any that we have mentioned.'

'Then the murderer must have left the coach?'

'He must; and that's where the difficulty comes in.'

'I know, but let us proceed. Our problem then really becomes – *how* did he leave the coach?'

'That's so, sir, and I have never been against anything stiffer.'

The chief paused in thought, as he absently selected and lit another cigar. At last he continued: 'Well, at any rate, it is clear he did not go through the roof or the floor, or any part of the fixed framing or sides. Therefore he must have gone in the usual way – through a door. Of these, there is one at each end and six at each side. He therefore went through one of these fourteen doors. Are you agreed, Inspector?'

'Certainly, sir.'

'Very good. Take the ends first. The vestibule doors were locked?'

'Yes, sir, at both ends of the coach. But I don't count that much. An ordinary carriage key opened them and the murderer would have had one.'

'Quite. Now, just go over again our reasons for thinking he did not escape to the sleeper.'

'Before the train stopped, sir, Miss Bintley, one of the three in the "Ladies Only," was looking out into the corridor, and the two sleeper attendants were at the near end of their coach. After the train stopped, all three ladies were in the corridor, and one attendant was at the sleeper vestibule. All these persons swear most positively that no one but the guard passed between Preston and the searching of the carriage.'

'What about these attendants? Are they reliable?'

'Wilcox has seventeen years' service, and Jeffries six, and both bear excellent characters. Both, naturally, came under suspicion of the murder, and I made the usual investigation. But there is not a scrap of evidence against them, and I am satisfied they are all right.'

'It certainly looks as if the murderer did not escape towards the sleeper.'

'I am positive of it. You see, sir, we have the testimony of two separate lots of witnesses, the ladies and the attendants. It is out of the question that these parties would agree to deceive the police. Conceivably one or other might, but not both.'

'Yes, that seems sound. What, then, about the other end – the third-class end?'

'At that end,' replied the inspector, 'were Mr and Mrs Smith with their sick child. They were in the corridor close by the vestibule door, and no one could have passed without their knowledge. I had the child examined, and its illness was genuine. The parents are quiet persons, of exemplary character, and again quite beyond suspicion. When they said no one but the guard had passed I believed them. However, I was not satisfied with that, and I examined every person that travelled in the third-class coach, and established two things: first, that no one was in it at the time it was searched who had not travelled in it from Preston; and secondly, that no one except the Smiths had left any of the compartments during the run between Preston and the emergency stop. That proves beyond question that no one left the first-class coach for the third after the tragedy.'

'What about the guard himself?'

'The guard is also a man of good character, but he is out of it, because he was seen by several passengers as well as the Smiths running through the third-class after the brakes were applied.'

'It is clear, then, the murderer must have got out through one of the twelve side doors. Take those on the compartment side first. The first, second, fifth and sixth compartments were occupied, therefore he could not have passed through them. That leaves the third and fourth doors. Could he have left by either of these?'

The Inspector shook his head.

'No, sir,' he answered, 'that is equally out of the question. You will recollect that two of the four men in the end compartment were looking out along the train from a few seconds after the murder until the stop. It would not have been possible to open a door and climb out on to the footboard without being seen by them. Guard Jones also looked out at that side of the van and saw no one. After the stop these same two men, as well as others, were on the ground, and all agree that none of these doors were opened at any time.'

'H'm,' mused the chief, 'that also seems conclusive, and it brings us definitely to the doors on the corridor side. As the guard arrived on the scene comparatively early, the murderer must have got out while the train was running at a fair speed. He must therefore have been clinging on to the outside of the coach while the guard was in the corridor working at the sliding doors. When the train stopped all attention was concentrated on the opposite, or compartment, side, and he could easily have dropped down and made off. What do you think of that theory, Inspector?'

'We went into that pretty thoroughly, sir. It was first objected that the blinds of the first and second compartments were raised too soon to give him time to get out without being seen. But I found that this was not valid. At least fifteen seconds must have elapsed before Miss Blair-Booth and the men in the end compartment raised their blinds, and that would easily have allowed him to lower the window, open the door, pass out, raise the window, shut the door, and crouch down on the footboard out of sight. I estimate also that nearly thirty seconds passed before Guard Jones looked out of the van at that side. As far as time goes he could have done what you suggest. But another thing shows he didn't. It appears that when Jones

22

ran through the third-class coach, while the train was stopping, Mr Smith, the man with the sick child, wondering what was wrong, attempted to follow him into the first-class. But the door slammed after the guard before the other could reach it, and, of course, the spring lock held it fast. Mr Smith therefore lowered the end corridor window and looked out ahead, and he states positively no one was on the footboard of the first-class. To see how far Mr Smith could be sure of this, on a dark night we ran the same carriage, lighted in the same way, over the same part of the line, and we found a figure crouching on the footboard was clearly visible from the window. It showed a dark mass against the lighted side of the cutting. When we remember that Mr Smith was specially looking out for something abnormal, I think we may accept his evidence.'

'You are right. It is convincing. And, of course, it is supported by the guard's own testimony. He also saw no one when he looked out of his van.'

'That is so, sir. And we found a crouching figure was visible from the van also, owing to the same cause – the lighted bank.'

'And the murderer could not have got out while the guard was passing through the third-class?'

'No, because the corridor blinds were raised before the guard looked out.'

The chief frowned.

'It is certainly puzzling,' he mused. There was silence for some moments, and then he spoke again.

'Could the murderer, immediately after firing the shots, have concealed himself in a lavatory and then, during the excitement of the stop, have slipped out unperceived through one of those corridor doors and, dropping on the line, moved quietly away?'

'No, sir, we went into that also. If he had hidden in a lavatory he could not have got out again. If he had gone towards the third-class the Smiths would have seen him, and the first-class corridor was under observation during the entire time from the arrival of the guard till the search. We have proved the ladies entered the corridor *immediately* the guard passed their compartment, and two of the four men in the end smoker were watching through their door till considerably after the ladies had come out.'

Again silence reigned while the chief smoked thoughtfully.

'The Coroner had some theory, you say?' he said at last.

'Yes, sir. He suggested the murderer might have, immediately after firing, got out of one of the doors on the corridor side – probably the end one – and from there climbed on the outside of the coach to some place from which he could not be seen from a window, dropping to the ground when the train stopped. He suggested the roof, the buffers, or the lower step. This seemed likely at first sight, and I therefore tried the experiment. But it was no good. The roof was out of the question. It was one of those high curved roofs – not a flat clerestory – and there was no hand-hold at the edge above the doors. The buffers were equally inaccessible. From the handle and guard of the end door to that above the buffer on the corner of the coach was seven feet two inches. That is to say, a man could not reach from one to the other, and there was nothing he could hold on to while passing along the step. The lower step was not possible either. In the first place it was divided – there was only a short step beneath each door – not a continuous board like the upper one – so that no one could pass along the lower while holding on to the upper, and secondly, I couldn't imagine anyone climbing down there, and knowing that the first platform they came to would sweep him off.'

'That is to say, Inspector, you have proved the murderer was in the coach at the time of the crime, that he was not in it when it was searched, and that he did not leave it in the interval. I don't know that that is a very creditable conclusion.'

'I know, sir. I regret it extremely, but that's the difficulty I have been up against from the start.'

The chief laid his hand on his subordinate's shoulder.

'It won't do,' he said kindly. 'It really won't do. You try again. Smoke over it, and I'll do the same, and come in and see me again tomorrow.'

But the conversation had really summed up the case justly. My Lady Nicotine brought no inspiration, and, as time passed without bringing to light any further facts, interest gradually waned till at last the affair took its place among the long list of unexplained crimes in the annals of New Scotland Yard.

★   ★   ★

And now I come to the singular coincidence referred to earlier whereby I, an obscure medical practitioner, came to learn the solution of this extraordinary mystery. With the case itself I had no connection, the details just given being taken from the official reports made at the time, to which I was allowed access in return for the information I brought. The affair happened in this way.

One evening just four weeks ago, as I lit my pipe after a long and tiring day, I received an urgent summons to the principal inn of the little village near which I practised. A motorcyclist had collided with a car at a cross-roads and had been picked up terribly injured. I saw almost at a glance that nothing could be done for him; in fact, his life was a matter of a few hours. He asked coolly how it was with him, and, in accordance with my custom in such cases, I told him, inquiring was there anyone he would like sent for. He looked me straight in the eyes and replied, 'Doctor, I want to make a statement. If I tell you will you keep it to yourself while I live and then inform the proper authorities and the public?'

'Why, yes,' I answered; 'but shall I not send for some of your friends or a clergyman?'

'No,' he said, 'I have no friends, and I have no use for parsons. You look a white man; I would rather tell you.'

I bowed and fixed him up as comfortably as possible, and he began, speaking slowly in a voice hardly above a whisper.

'I shall be brief for I feel my time is short. You remember some few years ago a Mr Horatio Llewelyn and his wife were murdered in a train on the North-Western some fifty miles south of Carlisle?'

I dimly remembered the case.

' "The sleeping car express mystery," the papers called it?' I asked.

'That's it,' he replied. 'They never solved the mystery and they never got the murderer. But he's going to pay now. I am he.'

I was horrified at the cool, deliberate way he spoke. Then I remembered that he was fighting death to make his confession and that, whatever my feelings, it was my business to hear and record it while yet there was time. I therefore sat down and said as gently as I could, 'Whatever you tell me I shall note carefully, and at the proper time shall inform the police.'

His eyes, which had watched me anxiously, showed relief.

'Thank you. I shall hurry. My name is Hubert Black, and I live at 24 Westbury Gardens, Hove. Until ten years and two months ago I lived at Bradford, and there I made the acquaintance of what I thought was the best and most wonderful girl on God's earth – Miss Gladys Wentworth. I was poor, but she was well off. I was diffident about approaching her, but she encouraged me till at last I took my courage in both hands and proposed. She agreed to marry me, but made it a condition our engagement was to be kept secret for a few days. I was so mad about her I would have agreed to anything she wanted, so I said nothing, though I could hardly behave like a sane man from joy.

'Some time before this I had come across Llewelyn, and he had been very friendly, and had seemed to like my company. One day we met Gladys, and I introduced him. I did not know till later that he had followed up the acquaintanceship.

'A week after my acceptance there was a big dance at Halifax. I was to have met Gladys there, but at the last moment I had a wire that my mother was seriously ill, and I had to go. On my return I got a cool little note from Gladys saying she was sorry, but our engagement had been a mistake, and I must consider it at an end. I made a few inquiries, and then I learnt what had been done. Give me some stuff, doctor; I'm going down.'

I poured out some brandy and held it to his lips.

'That's better,' he said, continuing with gasps and many pauses; 'Llewelyn, I found out, had been struck by Gladys for some time. He knew I was friends with her, and so he made up to me. He wanted the introduction I was fool enough to give him, as well as the chances of meeting her he would get with me. Then he met her when he knew I was at my work, and made hay while the sun shone. Gladys spotted what he was after, but she didn't know if he was serious. Then I proposed, and she thought she would hold me for fear the bigger fish would get off. Llewelyn was wealthy, you understand. She waited till the ball, then she hooked him, and I went overboard. Nice, wasn't it?'

I did not reply, and the man went on, 'Well, after that I just went mad. I lost my head, and went to Llewelyn, but he laughed in my face. I felt I wanted to knock his head off, but the butler happened by, so I couldn't go on and finish him then. I needn't try to describe the hell I went through – I couldn't anyway. But I was blind mad, and lived only for revenge. And then I got it. I followed them till I got a chance, and then I killed them. I shot them in that train. I shot her first and then, as he woke up and sprang up, I got him too.'

The man paused.

'Tell me the details,' I asked; and after a time he went on in a weaker voice.

'I had worked out a plan to get them in a train, and had followed them all through their honeymoon, but I never got a chance till then. This time the circumstances fell out to suit. I was behind him at Euston and heard him book to Carlisle, so I booked to Glasgow. I got into the next compartment. There was a talkative man there, and I tried to make a sort of alibi for myself by letting him think I would get out at Crewe. I did get out, but I got in again, and travelled on in the same compartment with the blinds down. No one knew I was there. I waited till we got to the top of Shap, for I thought I could get away easier in a thinly populated country. Then, when the time came, I fixed the compartment doors with wedges, and shot them both. I left the train and got clear of the railway, crossing the country till I came out on a road. I hid during the day and walked at night till after dark on the second evening I came to Carlisle. From there I went by rail quite openly. I was never suspected.'

He paused, exhausted, while the dread visitor hovered closer.

'Tell me,' I said, 'just a word. How did you get out of the train?'

He smiled faintly.

'Some more of your stuff,' he whispered; and when I had given him a second dose of brandy he went on feebly and with long pauses which I am not attempting to reproduce: 'I had worked the thing out beforehand. I thought if I could get out on the buffers while the train was running and before the alarm was raised, I should be safe. No one looking out of the windows could see me, and when the train stopped, as I knew it soon would, I could drop down and make off. The difficulty was to get from the corridor, to the buffers. I did it like this:

'I had brought about sixteen feet of fine, brown silk cord, and the same length of thin silk rope. When I got out at Crewe I moved to the corner of the coach and stood close to it by way of getting shelter to light a cigarette. Without anyone seeing what I was up to I slipped the end of the cord through the bracket handle above the buffers. Then I strolled to the nearest door, paying out the cord, but holding on to its two ends. I pretended to fumble at the door as if it was stiff to open, but all the time I was passing the cord through the handle-guard, and knotting the ends together. If you've followed me you'll understand this gave me a loop of fine silk connecting the handles at the corner and the door. It was the colour of the carriage, and was nearly invisible. Then I took my seat again.

'When the time came to do the job, I first wedged the corridor doors. Then I opened the outside window and drew in the end of the cord loop and tied the end of the rope to it. I pulled one side of the cord loop and so got the rope pulled through the corner bracket handle and back again to the window. Its being silk made it run easily, and without marking the bracket. Then I put an end of the rope through the handle-guard, and after pulling it tight, knotted the ends together. This gave me a loop of rope tightly stretched from the door to the corner.

'I opened the door and then pulled up the window. I let the door close up against a bit of wood I had brought. The wind kept it to, and the wood prevented it from shutting.

'Then I fired. As soon as I saw that both were hit I got outside. I kicked away the wood and shut the door. Then with the rope for handrail I stepped along the footboard to the buffers. I cut both the cord and the rope and drew them after me, and shoved them in my pocket. This removed all traces.

'When the train stopped I slipped down on the ground. The people were getting out at the other side so I had only to creep along close to the coaches till I got out of their light, then I climbed up the bank and escaped.'

The man had evidently made a desperate effort to finish, for as he ceased speaking his eyes closed, and in a few minutes he fell into a state of coma which shortly preceded his death.

After communicating with the police I set myself to carry out his second injunction, and this statement is the result.

MR PEMBERTON'S COMMISSION

Mr Courteney Pemberton, having placed his bag and rug on his reserved seat in the 8.25 a.m. Boulogne boat express, stepped down once more on the platform of the Gare du Nord in Paris in search of literature wherewith to beguile his journey.

Turning from the news barrow, Mr Pemberton's eyes met those of a young woman who was standing near. She was looking at him doubtfully, as if meditating speech. Her face was vaguely familiar, and Mr Pemberton, who was never averse to meeting charming young ladies, decided to claim acquaintance. But before he could take off his hat she withdrew her gaze; turned round and tripped off daintily down the platform.

Mr Pemberton gazed after her. She was small, dark and piquant and her face was adorable. With a happier expression he felt that in her cheeks there might on occasion be dimples, but now she looked worried and sad. Though quietly, even sombrely dressed, from the top of her small, close fitting hat to the tips of her tiny, high-heeled shoes, she was a vision to hold the eyes of any man.

'How these Frenchwomen can dress!' he thought, as, after watching her out of sight, he slowly climbed the steps of his carriage.

Mr Pemberton was a bachelor, stout, small of stature and successful. Formerly a City clerk, he had early found an outlet for his special talents in company promoting, and by means of a number of brilliant experiments with other people's money, had now achieved an assured position and a five figure income.

Though secure of a good deal more than his necessary bread and cheese, he had not yet gone out of harness. He was in fact even now returning from a bi-monthly meeting of French financial associates. Every first and third Tuesday of the month he spent with his colleagues, and the Wednesday morning following saw his departure from the Gare du Nord on his way back to England.

For a moment after the train started the face of the young Frenchwoman remained in Mr Pemberton's mind. He wondered where he could have seen her. But soon he turned his attention to his papers, until some time later the incident was recalled to his memory.

Returning along the corridor from lunch, he saw the girl for the second time. Again her face seemed familiar and again she was regarding him with doubt and hesitation. But this time she spoke, in what seemed to him the most entrancing voice to which he had ever listened.

'Pardon, monsieur, that I thus intrude myself on your notice. I am in vair' great trouble, but when I behold M. Pemberton I think to myself: it may be that he will aid me. Will monsieur permit that I beg of him a great favour?'

'You know me, mademoiselle?' Mr Pemberton returned in surprise, delighted at the prospect of an adventure after his own heart.

'But, yes, monsieur, though, alas, you do not know me. I am maid to Mme Hill-Brooke. Many times have I seen you at her house.'

He recalled her now. Mrs Hill-Brooke was a wealthy neighbour who lived in one of the finest of the older Hampstead houses, and he remembered having seen this girl on her drive on certain occasions when he had been to call.

'I remember you, of course,' he smiled, though his hopes of amatory adventure diminished. 'Yes? I'm sorry to hear you are in trouble. Tell me about it.'

'Monsieur is too kind. The last two weeks I stay with madame in Paris, but last night she leave to visit at Aix. She tell me to go back to London today to Mme Bowater. Monsieur without doubt knows Mme Bowater, madame's daughter?'

Mr Pemberton recalled Mrs Hill-Brooke's large and rather overbearing daughter, who lived near Hendon.

'Yes, of course,' he answered. 'I know her well.'

'Before madame leave last night,' resumed the young woman, 'she give me parcel to take to London. "Here, Denise," she say, "here is a gift for my grandchild." That is Mme Bowater's little girl, monsieur understands? "It is a little necklace and I want her to have it for her birthday party." That, monsieur, is tonight.'

Mr Pemberton had also seen the child, Hermione Bowater. He thought how characteristic of her grandmother was this action. Mrs Hill-Brooke idolized the little girl and Mr Pemberton felt that the gift of the necklace was a kindness which would have delighted the old lady, even more than her granddaughter.

'Yes?' he said encouragingly as the girl paused.

'Just before I leave the hotel this morning,' she resumed, 'I get a telegram.' She took a scrap of paper from her handbag. 'It is from the sister of my fiancé, and as monsieur see' – her dark eyes filled with tears – 'it tell that my fiancé has met with a vair' serious accident. It is that his life may be in danger.'

Mr Pemberton took the message. It had been handed in at Boulogne on the previous evening and received early that morning in Paris. It was in French and read: 'Jean seriously injured in motor accident. Come.'

He glanced at the girl. She was certainly very much upset, though evidently striving for composure. As he looked, a tear escaped from her eye and rolled slowly down her cheek. She hurriedly wiped it away.

'I am sorry,' he said, and his voice took on something more than a fatherly tone. She certainly was extremely pretty. 'And then?'

'Monsieur without doubt perceives my difficulty. It is that I desire to stay at Boulogne, but this package it requires me instead to go to England. If madame were here she would grant the permission – I know it. But she is not here: I cannot ask her. And madame would be so greatly distressed if the young lady was disappointed.' She broke off and her shrug was eloquent of despair.

'And you want me to take it across for you?' Mr Pemberton suggested softly.

The girl's face lit up and her eyes sparkled. 'Oh, if monsieur would but be so kind!' She smiled gratefully. 'It would give him but little trouble. I would telephone from Boulogne to Parker to visit at monsieur's house for it at six o'clock tonight. It would just be in time. Would six suit monsieur?'

Mr Pemberton knew Parker, Mrs Hill-Brooke's elderly and highly respectable chauffeur. He really did not see why he should not oblige the girl. As she said, it would give him no trouble. Indeed it would probably please Mrs Hill-Brooke, who was, he knew, exceedingly considerate to her servants.

'I'll take it with pleasure,' he said, gazing admiringly into his companion's dark liquid eyes. 'I shall be glad to help you, and I hope you'll find your fiancé better than you expect.'

Her eyes shone. 'Oh, monsieur! But how kind! Oh, how can I thank monsieur?'

As she spoke she took from her handbag a small parcel, sealed in an envelope and endorsed in what Mr Pemberton recognized was Mrs Hill-Brooke's handwriting: 'Miss Hermione Bowater, with love from Grannie.' He slipped it into the breast pocket of his inner coat, and after as long and intimate a conversation as he dared, returned to his own compartment, followed by the girl's exuberant thanks.

Mr Pemberton was what is commonly called a climber. Money had been his first object. He had made it in ways which he now found convenient to forget. But he had placed himself beyond the reach of financial embarrassment. Money had ceased to be his goal and social success had taken its place. From this point of view he valued his acquaintanceship with Mrs Hill-Brooke and her daughter. This episode of the child's, present might even be useful if it gave him an excuse for a more intimate interview than he had yet achieved.

★   ★   ★

He reached his home in Hampstead as the dark November evening was drawing in. There he took an early opportunity of locking the little parcel in his safe. Shortly before six he was seated in his library, running through the pile of correspondence which awaited him. For several minutes he worked, then suddenly he heard the sound of a car passing the window, followed by that of a distant bell.

'Parker, a trifle before his time,' he thought. There was a tramp of footsteps and a knock came to the library door. But when in answer to his invitation it was flung open he received a surprise.

'Detective Inspector French,' the butler announced, and a rather short man with a pleasant expression and blue eyes entered, followed by two companions. One was obviously a police officer in plain clothes, the other a slim man in a blue lounge suit.

'Mr Courtney Pemberton?' French said politely. 'I'm sorry for this intrusion, but I want a word with you, if you please.'

'Certainly Inspector. Won't you find seats?'

The trio subsided on to three chairs and French continued: 'I have been sent from Scotland Yard to make some inquiries about a package which it is alleged you received from Mrs Hill-Brooke's maid in the Boulogne boat train today.'

A sudden sense of impending ill came over Mr Pemberton. 'Yes?' he said uneasily. 'What about it?'

'May I ask, sir, if you have the package still?'

'I certainly have. But your questions alarm me. I hope nothing is wrong?'

French seemed relieved. 'There's not so much wrong if the parcel is safe,' he declared. 'Have you opened it?'

'Of course not. It's sealed and addressed to Mrs Hill-Brooke's little granddaughter. The maid said Parker would call for it at six o'clock tonight.'

'Parker?'

'Mrs Hill-Brooke's chauffeur.'

A light seemed to dawn on French. 'That's the link we want,' he replied in satisfied tones, glancing at his subordinate, who nodded obsequiously. 'I may admit, sir, we didn't see where you came in.'

'But I don't understand – ' Mr Pemberton was beginning, when the other interrupted him.

'Of course you don't, sir, but I'll explain in a moment. In the meantime I'll be glad if you'd tell me all you know of the affair.'

Mr Pemberton recounted his experiences, to which the trio listened with close attention.

'It's clear enough,' French commented when he had finished. 'Now I'll tell you something you didn't know. You were not carrying a gift from Mrs Hill-Brooke to her granddaughter. It was something more valuable even than that. You didn't imagine, sir, that that little package that Denise Marchant gave you was worth not less than twelve thousand pounds?'

Mr Pemberton stared. 'Bless my soul!' he exclaimed. 'Twelve thousand pounds! What on earth do you mean?'

'I'll tell you, sir. Mrs Hill-Brooke had a wonderful jade necklace. You've heard of it?'

At the mention of the necklace Mr Pemberton's heart fluttered. 'Heard of it?' he exclaimed. 'Everyone has heard of it. Yes, and I've seen it again and again.'

'I dare say. Well, sir, here's something else you didn't know. The necklace has been stolen.'

Mr Pemberton was appalled. 'Good heavens! Stolen!' he echoed in dismay. 'Not surely by that girl? I can scarcely believe it. She looked so – so innocent.'

A twinkle showed in the Inspector's blue eyes. 'I can believe it all right,' he declared dryly. 'She was a thief for all her looks. The necklace was stolen from Mrs Hill-Brooke's hotel in Paris last night. The girl, Denise Marchant, who has since been recognized as a well-known international thief hailing from Chicago, drugged her mistress and got away with it, at least, so we believe. She was traced to the Gare du Nord and arrested as she stepped from the boat train at Boulogne. A search showed that she had managed to get rid of the necklace, and a passing train official happened to have noticed her handing a package to you in a second-class compartment. Your description was wired to the Yard. We missed you at Victoria, but afterwards found your taxi and so traced you here.'

Mr Pemberton swore. 'You horrify me,' he exclaimed. 'What an unlucky chance that I should have been on the train!'

'That's the one point I'm not satisfied about,' French declared. 'All that business of the telegram about her fiancé shows premeditation. It looks to me more like as if they knew you would be there and arranged to use you. Did you tell anyone you were going?'

'No, but I take that journey twice a month – every first and third Wednesday.'

'That's it. They knew your movements and thought that you would make a safe messenger. We shall wait here till that chauffeur comes and get hold of him. In the meantime, I should be obliged if you would let us have a look at the necklace to make sure that it's all right.'

The financier nodded and crossed the room to his safe. Suddenly he recalled a point he had forgotten.

'Look here,' he exclaimed as he took out the package and placed it on the table before French, 'it's addressed in Mrs Hill-Brooke's handwriting. How do you account for that?'

French took a lens from his pocket and examined the spidery calligraphy.

'I don't know Mrs Hill-Brooke's hand myself, sir,' he said at last, 'but I know enough to tell you that this is not it. Anyone could see this is a forgery. Look for yourself. Those lines have not the smooth curves you get with genuine writing. They are a mass of tiny shakes. They have been drawn slowly from a copy.'

Mr Pemberton was soon convinced, and disgustedly he watched while the Inspector slit open the envelope and brought to light a magnificent necklace of green stones.

'That's it right enough,' French said in satisfied tones, beginning laboriously to count the beads. 'There should be seventy-two. And there are. That's it all right, I take it, Mr Hobbs?' He handed it to the slim young man. 'Mr Hobbs, of Devereux in Bond Street, who supplied the necklace,' he explained to Mr Pemberton.

Hobbs examined the lustrous rope for some minutes without speaking. Indeed, so long did his inspection last that French became impatient.

'Well, what's the matter? It shouldn't be hard to identify.'

The young man pored over it for some minutes longer, then replaced it on the table. 'It's not so easy to identify,' he said slowly, 'because I've never seen it before. It's not Mrs Hill-Brooke's necklace.'

French sprang to his feet with an oath, while Mr Pemberton stiffened suddenly.

'Not the necklace?' the former cried. 'Good heavens, man, are you sure?'

The slim young man nodded deliberately. 'I'm quite sure. And what's more, it's not a jade necklace at all. It's only glass. Worth about five shillings.'

French's jaw dropped. 'A fake!' he murmured, sitting down heavily and staring at the gleaming bauble. There was silence for a few moments, then French said bitterly: 'They're a smarter crowd than we reckoned on. Well, sir, I must ring up the Yard. I suppose I may use your phone?'

He put through his call, then, returning to the table, he picked up the envelope and absent mindedly looked at the seals. With a slight frown he took it close to the light and began scrutinizing it with his lens. Finally he glanced questioningly at Mr Pemberton.

'You say, sir, you didn't open this package?' he asked, and his tone was distinctly less suave.

'I certainly did not.'

'Then how do you explain the fact that it has been carefully opened and resealed?'

'Good heavens, Inspector! How should I know? I can only tell it wasn't done since I got it.'

'Look at these seals, Mr Pemberton. They have been detached from the lower paper and stuck on again in just not quite the same place.'

Once again Mr Pemberton felt a sense of impending ill.

'This introduces an unpleasant factor,' French went on gravely. 'The package has been opened and so far as we know it has been held only by Denise Marchant and yourself. If, as we believe, Marchant made it up and forged the address to deceive you, it's not easy to see why she should have opened it again. If she had wanted to put in a fake necklace she would have done it in the first instance. The suggestion is obvious.'

Mr Pemberton oscillated between anger and dismay. 'I have told you everything I know,' he retorted. 'I suppose you are hardly going to accuse me of stealing the thing?'

'I am not accusing you of anything, but the circumstances are such that you will have to satisfy me. You must see that a good deal of the evidence is against you.'

'Really, Inspector, this is perfectly scandalous,' Mr Pemberton declared angrily. 'You are making abominable insinuations without an iota of real evidence. I advise you to be careful. I have influential friends – '

French held up his hand. 'Now, sir, it won't do you any good to take that line. In your own interest you should be anxious to assist me. What I propose is that you come with me to the Yard and make your statement to the Chief Inspector. I am sure, sir, that it will prove a mere matter of form.'

Mr Pemberton was growing more and more uncomfortable. He recognized now the undistinguished part he had played in the affair. The fair Denise had, so to speak, drawn him, a corpulent and complaisant red herring, across the trail. He swore under his breath as he recalled with rueful admiration the girl's beauty, her appealing, innocent eyes, her real tears. 'Ugh!' he thought disgustedly, 'they're all the same. There's not one of them you can trust.' It was not the first time Mr Pemberton had intervened to assist lovely women in distress, and he had usually come to regret it. He turned back to French.

'How will my going to the Yard affect the matter?' he said indignantly. 'I can tell the Chief Inspector nothing more than I've told you. I – '

He was interrupted by the telephone, a long strident ring. He picked up the receiver.

'Mr Pemberton speaking,' he said, then passed the instrument over to French. 'It's the Yard.'

French listened, spoke, listened again. Then a change came over his manner. He put down the receiver and turned to the financier.

'Mr Pemberton, sir,' he declared in apologetic tones, 'it is my duty to tell you that in all good faith I have made a serious mistake. The Yard phones me that news has just come in from Paris. The necklace has been recovered. It was found in Paris in the possession of a man, evidently a confederate. The girl, Marchant, had managed to pass it on before she reached the station and she used you to lay a false trail. There remains therefore nothing but to offer my

41

sincere apologies and, if I may, to say how pleased I am that the matter is closed so far as you are concerned.'

Mr Pemberton was so relieved that he forebore to take a lofty tone.

'My word, Inspector, I'm glad to hear that. I thought you were going to give me no end of trouble.'

'I was only doing what I thought was my duty, sir,' French returned. 'Happily there's no chance now of your being annoyed. All the same, I regret that I have not yet quite finished. I must ask you for a signed statement about your interview with Denise Marchant. You will understand that this is necessary to enable the French police to get a conviction against her.'

'Right, Inspector,' Mr Pemberton returned, now once again in an excellent humour. 'But you don't expect me to write it all out, do you?'

'I'll do the writing, sir, if you will kindly sign it. It'll only take a minute or two.'

As a matter of fact it took twenty, but Mr Pemberton did not grudge the time. At last it was finished and he signed.

'I suppose, sir, you'd like to keep the faked necklace as a memento?' French went on. 'I should have asked you for it if the thieves were not known, but as they are we don't want it. But with your permission I'll take the outside paper. It may help to get a conviction.'

Mr Pemberton thought the necklace might make a good peg whereon to hang his story, and after watching Hobbs roll it up in its soft inside wrapping, he took it from him and locked it once more in his safe.

French got up. 'Your number, sir, if you please, in case we should want to phone you.'

After dinner Mr Pemberton rang up Mrs Hill-Brooke's daughter, Mrs Bowater, to congratulate her on the recovery of the necklace.

'Oh,' Mrs Bowater cried, 'how splendid! I hadn't heard. Mother rang me up about the loss, but they hadn't found it at that time. How did you hear?'

'The news has only just come through to Scotland Yard,' Mr Pemberton explained, 'so that you would scarcely have had time to hear it yet. As to my connection with the affair, it's a long story. If you'll be there tomorrow I should like to go over in the afternoon and tell you about it.'

'Please do,' Mrs Bowater invited, and rang off.

★   ★   ★

Mr Pemberton left his office early next day and drove out to Hendon. Mrs Bowater greeted him pleasantly, but he could see that she had something on her mind.

'That was a curious business last night, your telling me the necklace had been found,' she began at once. 'How did you say you knew?'

'Scotland Yard rang up the police officer who came to interview me on the subject,' Mr Pemberton returned. 'He repeated the message to me.'

'But it wasn't true,' declared Mrs Bowater.

'It wasn't true?' Mr Pemberton repeated. 'What wasn't true? I don't follow.'

'They haven't got the necklace. I expected to hear from mother, and when no message came I rang her up. The Yard must have made some mistake.'

Mr Pemberton was a good deal surprised. 'I suppose they must,' he repeated slowly. 'I haven't a great deal of faith in them, but I must say I shouldn't have expected them to go wrong on a matter of that kind.'

'No,' she said, 'it's strange, isn't it?'

'If you'll let me use your telephone I'll ring them up now and see what they have to say about it.'

Presently he got the Yard.

'Is Inspector French in the building?' he asked, and then, 'Tell him Mr Courtney Pemberton wants to speak to him.'

After a short silence came a voice, 'Inspector French speaking.'

'I say, Inspector,' went on Mr Pemberton, 'your people were wrong about the necklace. Mrs Bowater tells me she heard from Paris today and it hasn't been recovered.'

'What necklace, sir?' came the unexpected reply. 'I don't follow you.'

'Why, man, the necklace we discussed last night when you were in with me. What else could it be?'

'Some mistake, sir. You've got hold of the wrong man. I was here all last evening.'

Mr Pemberton's heart seemed suddenly to lose a beat.

'But, my goodness, Inspector, you gave me your card. "Inspector Joseph French, CID" Is there another Inspector French at the Yard?'

'No, sir, there's been a mistake. Will you tell me the circumstances?'

Mr Pemberton did so briefly. From what he could judge of his voice the Inspector seemed impressed.

'I think, sir,' the voice went on, 'I should like to see you about this. Where are you speaking from?'

Mr Pemberton told him.

'Then I shall go out there at once. I'm afraid, sir, you've been hoodwinked.'

With a sinking at his heart Mr Pemberton reported this new development to his hostess, adding a carefully bowdlerized account of his interview with Denise. Presently Inspector French was announced.

Though Mr Pemberton by this time was prepared for it, the Inspector's appearance gave him something of a shock. This was not the man who had called on him the previous evening!

'Now, sir,' said the new arrival gravely, 'I should be glad if you'd tell me the whole story.'

For the second time in half an hour Mr Pemberton related his adventure. When he had finished French nodded.

'It's as I thought, sir. You've been hoaxed. Have you got the necklace about you?'

'It's here. I brought it to show to Mrs Bowater, but we were so taken up discussing the affair that I forgot to do so.'

Mr Pemberton took the little parcel from his pocket. 'It's a perfectly splendid-looking piece of work,' he declared as he unwrapped the paper. 'No one but an expert would imagine it wasn't genuine. See.' He held it out.

Then suddenly he drew it back. He stared fixedly at it while slowly his eyes grew round and an expression of incredulous amazement became stamped on his features. For a time he seemed unable to speak, then he gave a hoarse cry. 'Bless my soul! It's not the same!'

'Ah,' said French with interest, 'now we're getting to it. Not the same as what?'

'As the one I brought across the Channel! This is quite different; a poor thing. The other was magnificent!'

French seemed pleased. 'I think that about clears it up, sir,' he declared. 'Tell me, did you happen to notice if my namesake had a scar on his temple near the hair?'

Mr Pemberton looked up in surprise. 'Why, yes, Inspector, he had. How on earth did you know that?'

A slow smile dawned on the other's face. 'Because I know who it was, and the others also. They're the Boston gang, and they're wanted by half the police in Europe as well as America. They'll not give us the slip this time. Excuse me while I phone the Yard.'

'But *he* phoned the Yard,' Mr Pemberton persisted.

Again French smiled. 'An old trick, Mr Pemberton. Anyone can lift the receiver without letting up the switch. Then you can talk till you're blue in the face and nobody hears you.'

The gang, French explained later, consisted of the girl and four men, and made a speciality of theft by ingenious tricks.

'We'll have to find out from Mrs Hill-Brooke about the details from her end, but apart from that the thing is pretty clear. I may tell you now that the Yard was advised from Paris of the theft. The necklace is well known and a pretty complete description of it was available. It was believed it would find its way to London as the best place in which to get rid of such stuff. As a matter of fact we're already looking out for it.'

As Mr Pemberton listened to this calm exposition, rage struggled with dismay in his mind. He certainly had been hoaxed – doubly hoaxed! The very men who were explaining to him how he had been hoaxed were themselves at that moment hoaxing him. 'Denise Marchant,' 'Inspector French,' 'Mr Hobbs,' the dummy policeman; Mr Pemberton choked as he thought of them.

'For goodness' sake explain the thing,' he stuttered.

'It's clear enough, as I said,' French returned. 'Speaking subject to later correction, I imagine a good deal of what my namesake told you was true. The girl, who had probably got her job by means of forged testimonials, stole the necklace during the night. Mrs Hill-Brooke was in the habit of taking a cup of hot milk just before getting into bed, and

Denise drugged this. Mrs Hill-Brooke slept so soundly that Denise was able to enter her room, take her keys from beneath her pillow, abstract the necklace and return the keys. One of her confederates sent her the telegram from Boulogne and with it she left by the 8.25.

'But she was up against a difficulty. She realized that the loss and her flight would be discovered early in the morning. If so, the services to England would be watched and she would certainly be taken at one of the ports. Hence she must get rid of her incriminating parcel. The same difficulty obtained in the case of the other members of the gang, so it would not do to pass the necklace to them. You, Mr Pemberton, became to her a gift from the gods. She knew of your bi-monthly journey and determined to use it. She approached you with her sad tale of an injured fiancé and managed to get you to undertake the carriage of the necklace. At Boulogne she simply disappeared and has not been heard of since.

'But the solution of this first problem raised a second. You had been given the necklace: how was it to be got back from you? I think you must admit the solution was worthy of the problem. A bogus inspector from Scotland Yard was an old enough idea, but it was effective. The man they called Hobbs is light-fingered; he began as a sneak thief in New York. He is an expert conjurer; he learned it as an aid to business. What he did was clear enough. He substituted the mock for the real necklace, probably while you were signing your statement. You say he returned it to you rolled in its inner paper?'

'Yes,' said Mr Pemberton, 'before my eyes. I saw the green stones being rolled up. I would have sworn they were what I brought from France.'

'All the same, sir, my double was careful to dull your critical faculties by suggesting the possibility of a criminal charge against you. That was to fill your mind with something else. Quite an astute move! Then the remaining member rang up as if from the Yard, and that gave them the excuse to decamp. Well, we can but hope for the best.'

But unhappily for Mrs Hill-Brooke, French's hopes were doomed to disappointment. Neither Denise nor her associates were ever heard of again. Some fine jade beads did indeed come on to the market, but no connection between them and the necklace could be proved.

THE GREUZE

Mr Nicholas Lumley, commission agent, laid his fountain-pen on his desk, straightened himself up with a sigh of relief, and glanced at his watch. To his satisfaction, it told him that the close of what had been a hard day's work had been reached, and that in a few moments he must leave his office if he wished to catch his usual train home.

But Fate ruled otherwise. As he rose from his desk an office boy entered and laid a card before him. It appeared that Mr Silas S Snaith, of 105 Hall's Building, Broadway, NY, wished to see him.

'Show him in,' said Mr Lumley, stifling a sigh of disappointment.

Mr Snaith proved to be a tall, slim man of some five-and-thirty, with clear-cut, strongly-marked features and two very keen blue eyes, which danced over Mr Lumley and about the room as if to leave no detail of either unnoticed. He was well-dressed in dark clothes of American cut, but a huge ruby ring, and diamond sleeve links seemed to point to a large endowment of money than of taste. In his hand he carried a leather dispatch case of unusually larger dimensions, which he placed carefully on the floor beside the chair to which Mr Lumley pointed.

'Mr Nicholas Lumley?' he began, speaking with a drawl and slight American accent. 'Pleased to meet you, sir.'

He held out his hand, which Mr Lumley shook, murmuring his acknowledgments.

The other seated himself.

'You take on jobs for other people, I reckon,' he said; 'odd jobs – for a consideration?'

Mr Lumley admitted the impeachment.

'Why, then, I'd like if you would take on one for me. It's a short job, and easy in a way, and if you can put it through there'll be quite a little commission.'

'What is the job, Mr Snaith?'

'I'll take a minute or two to tell you. But first, you'll understand it's confidential.'

'Certainly. Most of my work is that.'

There was a hint of coldness in Mr Lumley's voice which the other sensed.

'That's all right. No need to get rattled. Have a cigar?'

He pulled two from his waistcoat pocket, holding one out. Mr Lumley accepted, and both men lit up.

'It's this way,' went on Snaith. 'I'm in lumber, and I've not done too badly – house in Fifth Avenue and all that. I've more spare time than I had, and you mightn't believe it, but the hobby I'm fondest of is pictures. I've toured Europe for the galleries alone, and a mighty fine time I had. And my own collection runs to quite a few dollars.

'A year last fall I struck a picture that fairly licked anything I'd seen before – at Poitiers, in France – and when I left that town the picture came too. It cost me a cool 15,000 dollars, but it was worth it. It was a Greuze, a small thing, not more than ten inches by a foot – just a girl's head – but a fair wonder. The man I bought it from told me it was one of a pair, and since that I've been looking out for the other one. And now, by heck, I've found it!'

Mr Snaith paused and drew on his cigar, which he held pipewise in the corner of his mouth.

'I went up to see your Lord Arthur Wentworth this trip – Wentworth Hall, Durham. My word, that's some place! I had business with him about some acres of trees; he holds land in N'Yark State. Well, he had to go to some other room to get a map of his domains, and I had a look round the study to pass the time till he came back – idle curiosity, as you might say. Well, I'll be beat to a frazzle if there, on the wall behind where I'd been sitting, wasn't hanging the companion picture. I'd seen photographs of it, so I knew. I reckoned it might be only a copy, so I nipped up and had a thorough good squint at it before his lordship came back. I thought it was the genu-ine thing, but I just wasn't plumb sure.

'I had time to take a couple of snaps of it with my pocket Kodak before his lordship came back. Then we got the lumber deal through. For all he's a member of the effete British aristocracy, and about as ro-bust as a wisp of hay at that, he's all awake is Lord Arthur. A hard nut, as maybe you'll find.

'I said nothing about the picture, but all the time I was figuring how to get wise to its genu-ineness. When I got back to London I went to the best man I knew in the trade – Frank L Mitchell, of Pall Mall. What Frank L Mitchell doesn't know about pictures wouldn't be worth hearing. I had him promise to go down and see the picture for me.

'He went the next day. He waited about till he saw his lordship and friends start out on a gunning stunt, then he went to the house and, with lubricating the butler's palm, got a look round inside. He saw the picture, and he's satisfied it's the real article. But he went one better than that. The holders of all these genu-ine pictures are known, and when he got back he looked up the records, and found that when the present lord's father purchased it fifty years ago it was recognized to be the real thing, and paid for as such.

'So that's bedrock. It's likely the present owner knows that, but, of course, it's not certain. Mitchell figures that bit of canvas is worth three thousand of your pounds – 15,000 dollars. Now, Mr Lumley, I want that picture, and I want you to get it for me.'

The American sat back and looked expectantly at Mr Lumley. The latter's interest, which had been aroused by his visitor's story, suddenly waned.

'That's easier said than done, I'm afraid,' he answered slowly. 'Ten to one his lordship won't sell.'

'I reckon he'll sell – on my terms. Note the connection.' Mr Snaith demonstrated on his fingers. 'Here you have a lord that's hard up – I got wise to that. It takes him all he can do to keep his end up. Three thousand may not be much, but it's a darned sight more than he can afford to drop for nothing. You say he'll not sell. I'll agree, and ask, Why not? Why, because he's a proud man. He's not going to have that space on his study wall to remind him and his friends and his servants what he's done. But that's where I come in.'

Mr Snaith picked up his dispatch case and, opening it carefully, drew out a tissue-covered object and laid it on Mr Lumley's desk. With thin, nervous fingers he unwrapped the paper, revealing to the commission agent's astonished gaze a small oil painting in a heavy and elaborate gilt frame.

It was a charming study of a girl's head; light, elegant, dainty work. She was beautiful; blue-eyed, creamy-complexioned, and with masses of red-gold hair. But it was not her beauty that held the observer. It was the soul that shone behind the face. She was looking up eagerly into the

52

distance, and with a half-smile on her lips, as if at a vision
of heaven or love. Mr Lumley gazed in admiration.

'Warm stuff,' murmured Snaith appreciatively; 'and
that's only a copy. The picture's celebrated the world over,
and there's scores of copies. It's so good, is this one' – he
shot a side glance at Mr Lumley – 'I can hardly tell it isn't
genu-ine, and I doubt if you or Lord Wentworth could
either.'

Mr Lumley felt slightly uncomfortable, though he could
not say exactly why. But something faintly unpleasant in his
visitor's manner grated on his rather sensitive nerves.

'Now, my proposition is this,' the American went on.
'You see his lordship and show him this picture. Tell him
straight it's a copy, but so good a copy that only a few men
in the world could tell the difference. That he'll be able to
see for himself. Tell him your client offers him £2,000
down to let you change the pictures.'

'Why not deal with him yourself?'

'Two reasons. First, he don't love me any over that
lumber deal. He was polite and all that, but I could sense
he was glad to see my back. Secondly, I have business in
Paris to morrow, and I'll only have time to call here passing
through London on my way to the States next Friday.'

Mr Lumley did not reply, and Snaith continued,
speaking earnestly, 'He'll do it, for he wants the money.
Note how it would seem to him. No one will know anything
about it, and the new picture will look the same as the
other, and if the question ever does come up, it will be
supposed a mistake was made fifty years ago when his
father bought it. His pride will be saved. And if two
thousand doesn't raise him, why, you can offer him three. I
just must have the thing, and I don't mind a hundred or
two one way or another. Your own fee, if you put it through,

to be what you name – say £200 and expenses – that is, if you think that's enough.'

'Enough?' cried Mr Lumley. 'More than enough.'

'That's all right. Then I reckon you'll take it on? Now about bona fides. I've inquired about you before I came here, and what I've heard has satisfied me. But you know nothing of me, so you'll likely want some money instead of an introduction. As a guarantee of good faith I'll hand you notes for £2,000. If the deal comes to more you can pay it. You'll have the picture as security, and you can hold it till I pay you the balance. That all right?'

Mr Lumley thought rapidly. The business appeared simple and straightforward and, so far as he could see, square. At all events his part of it was square. He would be perfectly open with Lord Arthur, and he would honestly try to effect the sale. He could but fail.

'That seems very fair, Mr Snaith. I'll do what I can.'

'Good. Then count those.'

The visitor took a roll of notes from his pocket and, dividing them, handed a bundle to his new agent. There were twenty of them, Bank of England notes, each value £100.

'Correct,' said Mr Lumley as he scribbled a receipt.

'There are two other things,' Snaith went on. 'First, I don't want my name mentioned to Lord Wentworth. As I say, we got across each other over that lumber deal, and there's no kind of sense in putting his back up at the start. Just say a rich American wants it. And next, note my movements for the next three days. I cross tonight to Paris, and the Hotel Angleterre will find me till Friday morning. I cross Friday, call here at six p.m. for the picture, and leave Euston by the American boat train at seven. Got that?'

'I follow you,' answered Mr Lumley. 'That gives me two days. I'll keep your case to carry the picture.'

When the American left, Mr Lumley remained seated at his desk, his mind busy with the somewhat unusual commission with which he had been entrusted. He had frequently been asked to buy pictures, but there was a peculiar feature in this case. That idea of substituting the copy was new in his experience. But it was certainly ingenious, and if Lord Arthur were really hard up, it was conceivable that it might tempt him to agree to the proposal. But apart from this novel feature, the matter seemed reasonable and above board enough. And yet Mr Lumley was not satisfied. He was, or believed himself to be, a judge of character, and all his instincts had bade him beware of this Snaith. He felt that it behoved him to be on his guard, and stories he had read of confidence tricks recurred disquietingly to his memory.

But he had undertaken the task, and it now no longer mattered whether he had been wise or foolish; he must get on with it. He saw that he had no time to lose, and eleven o'clock that night, therefore, found him moving out of King's Cross en route for the north. But like the king of old, his thoughts troubled him and he could not sleep. Whether it was due to the rather heavy supper he had eaten – Mr Lumley was slightly dyspeptic – he did not know, but a feeling of depression and foreboding weighed on his spirits.

Suddenly an idea shot into his mind. Those notes – Snaith had parted with them so easily – *were they forgeries?* Feverishly he took them from his pocket and examined them. No, they seemed all right, but he determined he would make sure. His first business in the morning would be to call at a bank in Durham and have them tested. And then a possible meaning of Snaith's actions flashed before him – a real thing before his half-nightmarish imaginings vanished as if they had been. As the idea sank into his horrified brain, Nicholas Lumley began to know temptation.

He had believed that the American's offer was a £200 commission on the completion of a sale. But he saw now that he had been mistaken. No sale had been contemplated. The thing was hideously clear. He had been offered, not £200 but £2,200, £3,200 – any sum almost that he liked to name – *to steal the picture!*

And, merciful heavens, how easy it would be! He had only to devise some scheme to get to the study with his case and arrange something – a telephone call, for example – to get his lordship out of the room. Twenty seconds would do the whole thing. He could change the pictures, complete his ostensible business, leave without haste, and – Three thousand two hundred pounds! Perhaps four thousand!

Four thousand pounds! Four thousand pounds skilfully invested meant anything up to £250 a year. Mr Lumley was not a rich man, and an additional £250 would just make the difference between continuous, wearing economy and ease.

'Oh God!' he groaned, as he wiped the cold sweat off his forehead.

And Snaith would say nothing. He would perhaps smile knowingly, but he would pay and take his picture and go.

He wrestled with it all night, and next morning his face was grim and set as he sallied forth from the hotel in which he had breakfasted in search of a bank. Here one of his fears was disposed of. The notes were genuine.

An hour later he stepped out of a taxi at the door of Wentworth Hall. On requesting an interview with his lordship, he was shown into a small sitting-room and asked to wait. After some minutes he was here joined by Lord Arthur, an elderly man, thin and a little stooped, whose face was lined, as if from care and suffering.

He looked like a man with an incurable disease, to whom life is a continuous burden. But there was no trace of bitterness about him, and his manner as he waved Mr Lumley to a chair was not only courteous in the extreme, but even kindly.

'I am a commission agent, as you may have seen from my card, Lord Arthur,' began Mr Lumley, 'and I have called on behalf of a wealthy American client to lay before you a proposal which I sincerely trust you will not consider objectionable. May I say, as explaining my own position, that I have been offered a handsome commission – no less than £200 – if my client's wishes can be met? You will understand, therefore' – Mr Lumley smiled slightly – 'how much I hope you will see your way at least to give the proposal your full consideration.'

Lord Arthur seemed pleased by his visitor's candour.

'I will certainly do that,' he replied pleasantly. 'What does your client want?'

For an answer, Mr Lumley opened the dispatch case and took from it Mr Snaith's picture.

'Good gracious!' cried Lord Arthur when the tissue paper had been unrolled. 'My Greuze! How did you get that?' He looked sharply, and with some suspicion, at his visitor.

Mr Lumley hastened to assuage his fears.

'It is not yours, Lord Arthur. It is only a copy. But I wish you would tell me what you think of it.'

The old gentleman bent over the frame.

'If I had not your assurance, I should swear it was mine,' he said at last. 'Why, the very frame is identical. Bring it into the study and let us compare.'

Mr Lumley, having folded back the paper and replaced the frame in its case, followed the owner of the house to a large, well-furnished, airy room, giving on the terrace before the entrance. Lord Arthur closed the door and directed his visitor's attention to the wall above the fireplace.

Though he knew what to expect, the latter could scarcely refrain from a start of astonishment, for there, to all intents and purposes, hung the veritable picture which had been given to him by Snaith.

'Put yours beside it,' Lord Arthur directed.

Mr Lumley obeyed, and held his picture on the wall next to the other. Both men gazed in silence. The two seemed absolutely identical; the most minute examination even of the very frames failed to discover any difference between them.

'I shouldn't have believed it,' Lord Arthur said after a prolonged scrutiny; and then, indicating a deep armchair before the fire, 'But sit down, won't you, and tell me all about it.'

Mr Lumley slipped his copy back in the case and sat down. 'My client,' he explained, 'is an enthusiastic collector. He has recently purchased the companion to this, and he is keenly anxious to get the original of this one also. He wondered whether by any chance you could be induced so far to oblige him as to accept this copy, together with whatever sum you cared to name – he suggested £2,000 – but whatever you thought fair, in exchange for the original.'

Lord Arthur stared.

'Upon my word,' he exclaimed, 'this is very extraordinary business.' He sat in thought for a few moments; then, with a little sidelong glance, asked, 'Suppose I said three thousand?'

'If you think that a fair figure, I am authorized to pay it.'

His lordship made a gesture of bewilderment.

'Extraordinary!' he repeated. 'And how does your client know that my picture is the original?'

'That, unfortunately, I cannot explain to your lordship, as I am not in his confidence. But I may say that he seemed perfectly satisfied on the point.'

'It's more than I am. I may tell you that I have always regarded that picture – my own, I mean – as a copy. And I don't think, even if it were the original, that it would be worth anything like what you say. My knowledge of pictures, I admit, is but slight, still, I should say that a thousand would be its outside price.'

'Then, Lord Arthur,' interjected Mr Lumley with a smile, 'would you allow me to change it for a thousand pounds?'

'I didn't say that. What I meant was that I should like an explanation of what seems to me a very peculiar proposal, to put it mildly. A man comes to me and offers me for a copy of a picture at least twice the outside value of the original. It sounds queer on the face of it, doesn't it?'

'But, Lord Arthur, you must remember that in such a case the intrinsic value of the picture may not represent its reasonable price. It may have an additional sentimental value. It may be an heirloom. You might not care to hang anything but an original on your walls. These are consider- ations which my client took into account. That they have a cash value would be recognized in any court of law.'

'Quite true,' Lord Arthur admitted. 'And,' he went on dryly, 'bearing these points in mind, suppose I accept your £2,000 for my copy, would you be satisfied?'

'More than satisfied. I should be grateful.'

'You said you had the money there?'

For answer, Mr Lumley laid the twenty £100 notes on the table. Lord Arthur took them up.

'You will excuse me, I'm sure, but the matter is so very extraordinary that I think I am entitled to ask, how do I know that these are genuine, and, if genuine, are not stolen?'

'Perfectly entitled, Lord Arthur. I would suggest that you send a man with them to your bank, and let the matter stand over until you receive his report.'

Lord Arthur did not reply, but moving over to his table, he wrote for a few seconds.

'Sign that, and you may take the picture,' he said.

The document read:

Received from Lord Arthur Wentworth, Wentworth Hall, the copy of Greuze's 'Une Jeune Fille' which up to now has hung on his study wall, in return for the copy of the same picture supplied him by the undersigned on this date, and in consideration of the sum of two thousand pounds (£2,000), which has been paid in Bank of England £100 notes, numbered A61753E to A61772E.

'I don't want to take your client's money on false pretences,' Lord Arthur went on, 'so if within a month he has satisfied himself that he has bought a copy, I will refund him his £2,000 and his picture on his returning my own. If he likes to pay this money for the exchange, I do not see why I should not accept it. But you must warn him from me that I think he is in error, and the responsibility must be his alone. At all events, may I say I think you have fairly earned your commission?'

Mr Lumley, having expressed his gratitude and satisfaction, signed the receipt for the picture, obtained another for the money, exchanged the pictures, packed his purchase in the case, and, greatly rejoicing, took his leave. He felt he had successfully carried out his commission while preserving his honour, and on both counts he was pleased.

As he sat smoking in the afternoon express to King's Cross, he wondered idly which of them – Snaith or Lord Arthur – held the correct view about the picture. In any case, it did not matter very much to him, Lumley. He had done what he was asked, he would give Snaith a true account of what had happened, claim his commission, and, so far as he was concerned, the incident would be closed.

And then occurred one of those singular coincidences which are supposed to take place only in books, but which, as a matter of fact, happen more frequently in real life. It chanced that at Grantham, Dobbs, the RA, got into the compartment which up till then Mr Lumley had occupied in solitary state. Now, Lumley had played golf with Dobbs and the two were on friendly terms.

They conversed on general topics for some minutes, and, then it occurred to Mr Lumley that it would be interesting to get Dobbs' opinion of the Greuze. He therefore opened his case and produced the picture.

'What do you think of that?' he asked, as he handed it over.

'Too dark to say,' returned the other, 'but it looks a jolly fine copy.'

'A copy?'

'A copy, yes. It's a well-known picture. Unless' – the RA smiled – 'unless you are just back from a burglarious expedition to Paris, the original is still in the Louvre.'

Mr Lumley gasped.

'I suppose, Dobbs,' he said earnestly, 'you're sure about that?'

'Of course I'm sure. Everyone knows that who knows anything at all of pictures. Why, I remember the exact place on the wall where it's hung. I've looked at it scores of times. You didn't by any chance think it was an original?'

'I know nothing about it, but I bought it for a man who thought so.'

'H'm. How much, if it's a fair question?'

'Two thousand.'

The RA stared.

'Good Lord, man!' he cried. 'You're not serious? The original of that picture is worth, perhaps £1,200. This' – he tapped the painting on his knee – 'is worth, well, say £40 at the outside limit.'

Mr Lumley felt the bottom dropping out of his world.

'I don't understand the thing any more than you do,' he answered slowly. 'I was commissioned to buy this particular picture. I was told I might give two thousand or three, or practically anything that was asked, but I was to get the thing.'

'I suppose it was a confidential deal?'

'Well, yes, I'm afraid so; but it would not be a breach of confidence to say it was for an American of the *nouveau riche* type.'

Dobbs tossed his head contemptuously.

'That explains it,' he said with a short laugh. And then the talk drifted into other channels.

But though Mr Lumley felt no responsibility for a mistake, had such been made, there still remained in his mind an uneasy feeling about the whole affair. And later on the same evening he made a discovery which perturbed him still further.

He was wrestling with the problem of how Snaith, a man who had visited most of the galleries in Europe, could have failed to know that the original was in the Louvre. And then he recollected that this puzzle was not confined to the American. Snaith had not trusted his own judgment. He had consulted the best authority on pictures of whom he knew in London – Mitchell of Pall Mall. Mitchell's name was unfamiliar to Mr Lumley, but at all events he must be an authority, and – Mitchell had not known either.

He wondered what kind of standing Mitchell possessed, and, after reaching his office and locking up the dispatch case in his safe, he took up his directory to see if he could gain any light on the point. And he did, but not the kind of light he expected. There was no one in Pall Mall of that name!

Mr Lumley whistled. From experiencing a slight dissatisfaction he was now thoroughly uneasy. It certainly looked as if something were wrong.

He locked his office and, with a feeling of gratified surprise at the manner in which he was rising to an unexpected emergency, he drove to one of the large hotels on the Embankment much frequented by wealthy Americans. Here he was able to borrow a directory of New York. He looked up Snaith. There was no Silas S Snaith mentioned either in Fifth Avenue or anywhere else. He looked up Hall's Building in Broadway. The name did not appear.

'Hoaxed!' Mr Lumley whispered to himself as he wiped the perspiration off his forehead. 'The whole thing's a plant. There is no Snaith. There is no Mitchell. That man's story was a yarn. But what in the name of goodness is the game?'

He sat on in the hotel reading-room buried in thought. And gradually little things, noted subconsciously at the time and forgotten, returned to his memory and became definite mental pictures. Though he had hardly realized it during the interview, Snaith had puzzled him – not Snaith's story, but Snaith himself, his personality. His language, his bearing, all, Mr Lumley now saw, had been inconsistent. At one time he had been ultra-American in an out-of-date sort of way; he had, for example, talked the American of the dime novel or the screen message, while at another his English had been as good as Mr Lumley's own. The more the commission agent thought over it the more suspicious he became that Snaith was concealing his identity – that he was not, in fact, an American at all.

As he turned the matter over in his mind a possible solution suddenly struck him. Could it be that Snaith meditated an attempt to steal the original from the Louvre? He had certainly spoken of a visit to Paris. Could his plan be to destroy Lord Arthur's picture, and to swear that the treasure that he had stolen had been purchased from his lordship? If so, he would be able to support his story by incontrovertible evidence of the sale. Yes, Mr Lumley concluded, this theory certainly represented a possibility.

And if so, there was the equal possibility that he, Lumley, was assisting in a crime. How could he test the matter? How satisfy himself?

He decided to go down to Scotland Yard, tell his story, and do what he was there advised. Responsibility for the sequel would then be off his shoulders.

He glanced at his watch. It was just ten o'clock. Leaving the hotel, he drove along the Embankment to the Yard.

'I want to see the Inspector on duty,' he demanded.

He was shown into a small office, and there a tall, quiet-mannered, efficient-looking man asked him his business.

'I have had, Mr Inspector, a somewhat unusual experience,' began Mr Lumley. 'I don't in the least know that anything is wrong, but the circumstances are suspicious, and I felt I ought to let your people know, so that you could form your own opinion.'

'Very right, sir. Perhaps you will tell me the facts.'

Mr Lumley began to recount his adventures. The Inspector listened courteously but impassively till Lord Arthur's name was mentioned. Then a sudden gleam of interest came into his eyes, and he gave his visitor his undivided attention. But he did not interrupt, allowing Mr Lumley to finish his story in his own way.

'You have made a very clear statement, sir,' he said when the other ceased speaking, 'and I should like to congratulate you on your wisdom in reporting to us. I think it probable that you'll find yourself justified. Excuse me a moment.'

He left the room, returning in a few minutes with another official, who carried a large file of papers.

'This is Inspector Niblock,' he said, 'and though I couldn't tell until I had heard it, I fancy he will be even more interested in your statement than I was. Would it be too much to ask you to repeat it to him?'

For the second time Mr Lumley related his experiences. While the first Inspector had shown interest in the story,

Niblock scarcely covered up actual excitement with the cloak of professional calm. He repeated his colleague's congratulations and then turned to the file of papers. From it he drew a number of photographs and handed them to Lumley.

'Have a look over those, sir, will you?' he invited.

Mr Lumley took the cards. They were portraits of a number of quite ordinary-looking men and women. Mildly surprised, he turned them over. And then his surprise became astonishment, for there, on the fourth card, was a full-length view of Mr Silas S Snaith.

'Seen him before?' asked Niblock, chuckling and rubbing his hands. 'I think you've done a better stroke of business than you know, Mr Lumley.' He became serious in a moment and continued, 'And now let us lay our plans, for there must be no bungling in this affair.'

The two Inspectors spoke in undertones for a few moments. Then Niblock turned.

'You say the picture is now in your safe, Mr Lumley? I presume it is in precisely the same state as when you took it down from Lord Arthur's study wall.'

'Precisely.'

'We must get hold of it at once. Will you come to your office now and let us have it? You can keep the taxi and drive on home.'

The three men left the great building and, hailing a vehicle, were driven to Mr Lumley's place of business. The latter led his companions to his private room where, after pulling down the blinds, he produced the dispatch case. In a moment the detectives were examining the picture.

'We'll borrow it as well as this case,' said Niblock as he carefully repacked it. 'You may expect us back with it at about five tomorrow. Where does that door lead to?'

'A filing-room.'

'The very thing. You can, perhaps, let us withdraw into that room, so that if your interview with Snaith does not go satisfactorily we shall be able to give you assistance. That's all tonight, I think.'

Mr Lumley begged for further information, but Niblock refused it on the ground that the agent's display of ignorance would be more convincing to Snaith if it were genuine.

'If,' the Inspector added, 'by some chance he should come before his time, you will tell him that the picture has been left at your bank for safe keeping, but that it will be in your hands before six. If we find him here on our arrival, we shall assume the role of bank officials. But in that case we shall have to wait in the passage outside your office.'

Next evening Mr Lumley was once more seated in his private room, when, shortly after five, the two Inspectors entered, accompanied by a sergeant in uniform.

'There is the picture,' said Niblock, after brief greetings had been exchanged, 'untouched, except that we have had to put it in a new frame. By an unfortunate accident I dropped it, with the result that the corner of the frame was split and the gilding damaged. You will see here what has happened.'

The Inspector undid a brown paper parcel and brought to light the old frame, split, as he had said, at one corner.

'Should Mr Snaith observe that the frame has been changed,' he continued, 'you will describe the accident, though saying it happened with yourself. You will express regret for your carelessness, and you will say that you kept the old frame for his inspection. You can leave the rest to us. Now let us into your filing-room, for you must be alone when your visitor comes.'

The three police officers stepped into the small back chamber, and the door was almost, but not completely closed. Mr Lumley, nervous and considerably perturbed, sat writing at his desk. He did not know what form the coming interview was to take, and he was considerably annoyed that the officers had not taken him more fully into their confidence. He felt that if he only knew what to expect he would be in a better position to meet it.

The minutes passed slowly – so slowly that more than once Mr Lumley put his watch to his ear to make sure that it was still ticking. But at last six o'clock came, and a few minutes later Mr Snaith was announced.

'Say, but your railroads want hustling some,' was his greeting as he stepped breezily into the room. 'I've just got in from Paris, only forty minutes late.' He sat down and opened his heavy coat, then went on with more than a trace of anxiety in his tone, 'And how has the deal gone? Got it through?'

'Got it through, Mr Snaith, I am glad to say, and with very little trouble. But one thing is rather upsetting. Lord Arthur says the picture isn't genuine – it's only a copy.'

Snaith looked up sharply.

'But you have it all right – here?' he asked, and in spite of an obvious effort, there was eagerness in his voice.

'Yes; it's in my safe. But when he said it was a copy, I was doubtful – '

'That's all right. I just thought he mightn't know. Don't worry yourself any. All you've to do is to give me the picture and get your money, and the deal's OK. What did you pay him?'

'Two thousand, but he said he would refund it if you found the picture was a copy and returned it within a month.'

'Did he so? Well now, that was vurry considerate of him. Let's have the thing, anyhow.'

Mr Lumley rose and, unlocking the safe, took from it the dispatch case and laid it on the desk before his visitor. With an eagerness that he could no longer control, Snaith withdrew the picture and, his hands trembling with excitement, tore off the tissue covering. For a moment he gazed at the picture with a gloating satisfaction; then his face changed.

'This is not it!' he cried sharply, and his eyes searched Mr Lumley's face with a look in which suspicion turned rapidly to menace. 'By the Lord, if you try to pull any stuff on me, I'll make you wish you had never been born! What's the meaning of it?'

Mr Lumley, fortified by the knowledge of the presence of his other visitors, took a more lofty one than he otherwise might have essayed.

'Really, Mr Snaith,' he answered in cold tones, 'you forget yourself. I am not accustomed to be spoken to in that way. When you apologize I'll continue the conversation, not before.'

For a moment it seemed as if Snaith would resort to violence. Then an idea seemed to strike him, and he controlled himself with an obvious effort and spoke again.

'No offence – no offence,' he growled irritably. 'You're so plaguey set on your dignity. But explain. That's not Lord Arthur's picture.'

'That *is* Lord Arthur's picture,' Mr Lumley asserted stoutly.

'Then you've been monkeying with it. It's not the frame.'

'It's not the frame, I know, and if you had been more civil I should express greater regret. As a matter of fact, I dropped the picture – most carelessly, I admit – but it slipped – '

Snaith's gaze had fixed itself on Mr Lumley with a dreadful intensity. At last, unable to control himself any longer, he burst out, 'Damn it all, man, get to the point, can't you! Where is the frame now?'

'It's here. As I was saying, I dropped the picture and damaged the corner of the frame. I got it reframed, but the old frame was sent back also.'

Mr Snaith sat back limply and wiped his forehead.

'Why the blazes couldn't you say so at once?' he growled. 'I'll have the old frame too.'

Mr Lumley turned back to his safe.

'There,' he said, quite rudely for him, 'I hope you're satisfied that's the right one.'

Snaith took the frame and examined it minutely. Then he turned it over and looked at the back. For a moment he remained motionless, then he hurled it on to the desk and sprang to his feet with an inarticulate snarl, his face livid with rage and disappointment.

'You thief!' he yelled with a bitter oath. 'You thief! If you don't shell out within ten seconds I'll send you straight to hell!' and the appalled Mr Lumley found himself gazing directly into the bore of an automatic pistol.

But at that moment there was an interruption. A quiet voice broke in conversationally, 'Now, none of that, Mr William Jenkins – none of that. It's on to you this time, I guess. Put the gun down and give in like a man when you're beaten.'

Snaith, thunderstruck, turned to see the two Inspectors covering him with their revolvers. His jaw dropped. For a moment it seemed as if he were going to show fight; then slowly his fingers relaxed and the pistol fell on the desk.

'The darbies, Hughes,' went on Niblock, 'and then we can put our toys away and have a chat.'

Snaith seemed utterly dumbfounded, and he made no resistance as the sergeant first pocketed the pistol and then handcuffed him.

When he was rendered harmless, Niblock turned to Mr Lumley.

'I'm sorry, sir,' he said courteously, 'for having had to submit you to this, but we had to let him demonstrate before witnesses that he was after the frame, and not the picture. Thanks to you, sir, he has done that pretty completely.' He turned to the prisoner. 'I have to warn you, Jenkins, that whatever you say may be used in evidence, but at the same time, if you wish to make a statement I will take it.'

The prisoner, apparently stupefied at the sudden turning of the tables, made no reply.

'In that case,' Niblock resumed, 'we had better get away. With your permission, we'll take the picture and frame, Mr Lumley, and later I'll call and explain anything that may still be puzzling you.'

*   *   *

Two days later Mr Lumley called at the yard in response to an invitation from Inspector Niblock. There he met the two Inspectors and their Chief, as well as Lord Arthur Wentworth. As Mr Lumley entered the room, the latter sprang to his feet and came forward with outstretched hand.

'And this is the man to whom I owe so much,' he cried warmly. 'Allow me, my dear sir, to express my great gratitude and appreciation of your actions.'

His lordship beamed as he pumped Mr Lumley's hand up and down.

'But,' said Mr Lumley in some embarrassment, 'I can assure you, Lord Arthur, that I am still in ignorance of what I have done.'

'You will soon know all about it. Tell him, Inspector. You are better up in the details than I.'

'Mr Lumley, sir,' began Niblock, leaning forward and tapping the desk with his forefinger, 'your friend, Mr Dobbs, valued that picture at about £40, and Snaith or Jenkins at £2,000 – to you at least.' The Inspector's voice became very impressive. 'They were both wrong. The actual value of that picture was something over five-and-forty thousand pounds!'

Mr Lumley gasped.

'And would you like to see what gave it its value?' went on Niblock, evidently relishing mightily the sensation he was creating. He opened a drawer in his desk, took out a little box, and out of it poured on to the table what seemed a stream of silvery light.

'Pearls! A necklace!' ejaculated Mr Lumley.

'A necklace, yes,' went on Niblock. 'More than that. *The* necklace. Lady Wentworth's celebrated pearl necklace, valued at £45,000, and which was stolen from her over six months ago.'

'I remember,' cried Mr Lumley helplessly. 'I read of it at the time. But how – ?' He looked his question.

'I'll tell you, sir. Some nine or ten months ago Lord Arthur took on a footman, a young man named William Jenkins. He proved himself a capable servant, and seemed eminently respectable and trustworthy. But he was your Silas S Snaith.

'Some three months after he arrived there was a big dance at Wentworth Hall, at which her ladyship intended to wear her necklace. Lord Arthur took it from his safe and handed it to her about 7 p.m. She did not wear it at dinner, which was a comparatively hurried affair, but left it in a drawer of her dressing-table. When she went up about 8.30 to dress for the ball it was gone.

'The alarm was immediately given, and a private detective, who was in attendance, took charge. Police were telephoned for and a ring was made round the house, and no one was allowed to leave unless vouched for. The guests were by this time arriving, but the matter was hushed up, and the dance went on.

'In the searching inquiry that followed suspicion at first fell on Jenkins, as being the newcomer. It was further shown that he was out of observation for five minutes between 7 and 8 p.m., in which time he could have visited Lady Wentworth's room. But it was also shown that he could not possibly have left the house nor communicated with an accomplice outside. Therefore, as none of the pearls had come into the market, we came to the conclusion that the thief had hidden them in some place about the house. But the most careful search failed to reveal them.

'You may understand then, sir,' Inspector Niblock continued, bowing to Mr Lumley, 'that when I heard that a man of the description of Jenkins was offering a large sum of money for a valueless picture from the study of Wentworth Hall, I became interested, and when you selected Jenkins from the Hall servants I became more interested still. My colleague and I got the picture from you, and we found that a groove had been cut right round the back of the frame and filled with putty, in which was embedded the necklace. We removed the pearls and fixed up that test with that frame, to make sure it was that he was after. I may say that Jenkins has confessed.

'It appears he is an old friend of Lucille, her ladyship's maid, and she had often spoken in his hearing about the necklace. He had determined to have a try for it, believing he could sell the pearls singly and in different places. He made friends with the butler, got his support, and so his job. He had decided he could never get directly away with the swag, so he looked round for a hiding place, eventually choosing the frame of this picture. The hiding place was prepared for weeks beforehand.

'On the evening of the dance Lucille told him the necklace was to be worn. He pumped her as to its resting-place, and while everyone was at dinner, he slipped up to her ladyship's room, snatched up the necklace, ran to the study, and hid it in the prepared hiding place.

'He lay low while the search continued, but three months later gave in his notice and left. He had then to find some way of getting the picture. He could not go to the Hall himself, as he would be known, and I think it really is not easy to devise a better plan than that he adopted.'

★   ★   ★

It remains only to be told that Mr Lumley shortly became the happy recipient of those same notes for £2,000 which he had handed to Lord Arthur, together with a cheque for the promised reward of £1,000, his lordship holding that of all concerned the commission agent had the best rights to the money.

THE LEVEL CROSSING

In spite of himself Dunstan Thwaite shivered as he looked at the level crossing. For here was where he intended, this very night, to kill his enemy, John Dunn.

It was a place well suited to his purpose. A sharp curve and some belts of firs screened both sight and sound of approaching trains. Speeds were high and with only four or five seconds' warning the least carelessness or hesitation might well prove fatal. An accident here would raise no suspicions.

The crossing, moreover, was private; no signalman in charge, no gatehouse near. Nor in that lonely country was it overlooked. The nearest house was Thwaite's own, and even from it the view was masked by trees. The lane which here crossed the railway ran up into the country behind Thwaite's house and joined the main road at the opposite side of the line. But the crossing was seldom used. Because of the danger there was practically no wheeled traffic and the gates were kept locked. Wickets were provided, used mostly by foot-passengers seeking a short cut to the neighbouring station. But of these there were few and at the time Thwaite had in mind there would be none.

As he had planned it there would be little difficulty in carrying out the crime. Nor was there the slightest chance of discovery. The thing was safe, safe as houses. Only a little care, an ugly few minutes, and he would be once more a free man.

For five years now John Dunn had been his tormentor. For five years he had suffered because he had seen no way of escape. Even his health had become threatened and he was reduced to sleeping draughts to get a night's rest. Now he was shedding his burden. After tonight he would be free.

The trouble was of Thwaite's making, though that did not make it any the easier to bear. Thwaite was a climber and so far a successful climber. Left an orphan, he early had had to fend for himself. By a lucky chance he had got a job in the office of a large steel works. There he had worked with a single aim. It had borne fruit. At the age of thirty-five he was appointed accountant. Had it not been for his one act of suicidal mania, he would have felt his future assured.

His break had occurred five years earlier when he was assistant to his elderly and easygoing predecessor. Thwaite was about to be married 'above him', as the silly phrase goes. The beautiful Miss Lorraine was not only one of the leaders of the local society, but was reputed to have a well-lined pocket. Why she proposed to 'throw herself away' on a man in Thwaite's position, none of her friends could imagine. Some said it was a romance of pure love, others more cynically, that she believed that she had backed a winner. For Thwaite at all events it promised to be a brilliant match, but he found it was going to be expensive. In fact, the preparations pressed him so hard that he was faced with the choice either of obtaining more ready money or of losing Hilda Lorraine. Then suddenly the opportunity had presented itself and Thwaite had lost his head. A bit of casual slackness on the part of one of the directors, instantly seized and turned to his own advantage, a little extraordinarily skilful manipulation of the books under the nose of his infirm superior, and a cool thousand of the firm's money found its way into Thwaite's pockets.

Needless to say, he had hoped to put it back after his marriage, but before he had time to do so the loss was discovered. Reason to suspect another clerk was discovered along with it. Nothing could actually be proved against the unfortunate man, but he was quietly got rid of.

Thwaite had sat tight and said nothing. He had got away with it – almost. No one knew, no one guessed, but his next in command, John Dunn. And Dunn wormed his way through the books till he got his proof.

But Dunn didn't use his knowledge, not in the way an honest clerk should. Instead he approached Thwaite secretly. A hundred pounds changed hands.

That hundred pounds, that and the knowledge of his power, satisfied Dunn for the first year. Then there had been a second interview. Thwaite had had a rise. Mrs Thwaite had brought money with her. Dunn went home with two hundred and fifty.

For five years it had gone on. Dunn's demands ever increasing and nothing to suggest they would ever cease. Nothing but the one thing, the remedy Thwaite was now going to take.

At first Thwaite had tried the obvious way of escape 'I suppose, Dunn,' he had said, 'it hasn't occurred to you that you're in the same boat yourself? You've known this thing and you've kept silent; you're an accessory after the fact. If you send me to prison you'll come with me.'

But Dunn had only laughed maliciously. 'Oh come now, Mr Thwaite,' he had answered, 'you ain't 'ardly doin' me justice, you ain't.' As if it was yesterday Thwaite remembered the mixture of mockery and cunning in the man's eyes. 'I'll only 'ave found it out the very day I make my report. See? I 'ad suspected it from the first, but I 'adn't been able to prove it. I'll tell 'em that that very day I was lookin' over the old ledger, an' there for the first time I'd seen the proof. No accessory about that, Mr Thwaite. Nothin' there but a poor clerk carryin' out a disagreeable dooty for the good of the firm.'

Thwaite had cursed; and paid. And now the fact was that after four years of married life he could no longer make ends meet. His wife indeed had brought money, but nothing like the sum with which rumour had credited her. Besides, she held that it was her husband's place to supply money. She demanded an expensive house, an expensive car, expensive servants, entertaining, suppers and theatres in town. Thwaite, moreover, had his own position to keep up. And he could not run to it, not with this continual drain to Dunn. With Dunn out of the way he could just manage.

'I went into Penborough yesterday and had a look at that Sirius saloon,' his wife had remarked a couple of nights before. 'It's a nice car, Dunstan. I don't see why we shouldn't have it now. If you're really so hard up as you pretend, we could get it on the hire purchase system.'

'I don't want to begin that,' Thwaite answered. 'With it you never know what you own or where you are.'

'You don't want it perhaps,' his wife returned sharply, 'but what about me? What about my going about in a shabby old Austin years out of date and all my friends turning up in Singers and Daimlers and Lincolns? Look at Myra Turner with her new Rolls Royce. I tell you I feel it. And I'm not going to stand it, what's more.'

'I know all about it, Hilda,' Thwaite said wearily. 'I know it's due to you and you shall have it in time. But we'll have to wait. Believe me, I haven't got the money.'

Her face took on the cold set look which he knew and dreaded. There had been many such discussions: 'I don't want to pry into your secrets,' she said in a hard cutting voice. 'Even if you're keeping up another establishment I don't ask about it. But I'll tell you this: if you don't order that car, I will. I don't see why your likes and dislikes should be considered, but not mine. You can at least meet the first instalment, I presume?'

Thwaite sighed. His lips were sealed because he knew that she had reason on her side. It was not shortage of money nor the inability to buy expensive cars that had turned a loyal comrade into a suspicious stranger and their happy home life into a nightmare. It was her want of confidence in him. It was the knowledge that he had several hundred a year for which he would not account. She was no fool, Hilda Thwaite, and his early attempts to throw dust in her eyes had only confirmed her suspicions. Yet he believed that but for this money trouble their old happy relations might be resumed. But that was where John Dunn came in.

Lord, how he hated the man! The thought of the level crossing recurred to him. It was no new idea. Weeks ago he had thought out the ghastly details of what might happen there. His scheme had had its inception when the doctor had ordered him sleeping draughts. He had thought first of giving the man a concentrated dose. Then he had seen that this was too crude and a subtler way had suggested itself. With the level crossing at hand an innocuous dose only would be required.

Thwaite let his mind dwell on the completed scheme. With something not far from horror he felt himself being driven towards it by forces greater than himself. Like the man in Poe's sketch he seemed to see the walls of his chamber closing in on him.

The very next morning, while Thwaite was still hesitating, Dunn himself had put the lid on the situation.

The two men were in Thwaite's private room, discussing some business.

'Sorry to trouble you, Mr Thwaite,' Dunn began in his whining voice when the firm's affair had been settled, 'but I'm in difficulty again about my son. 'E's got into more trouble and 'e must produce five 'undred or 'e'll get run in. I was wonderin', Mr Thwaite, if maybe you could 'elp me?'

For a reason known only to himself Dunn's demands always took the form of aid for a mythical son. On the first occasion when Thwaite had pointed out the flaw in this premise Dunn had cheerfully admitted it, but with cynical insolence his subsequent applications had been couched in the same terms.

'Damn your son!' Thwaite returned in low tones. Though the room was large he must be careful not to be overheard. 'Can you never say straight out what you want?'

'Straight as you like, Mr Thwaite,' the other agreed amicably. 'Just five 'undred quid. It ain't much from one gentleman to another.'

Thwaite felt a yearning to seize the creature and slowly to choke the life from his miserable body.

'Five hundred?' he repeated. 'You wouldn't like the moon by any chance? Because you're as likely to get the one as the other.'

Dunn washed his hands in air. 'Oh, come now, Mr Thwaite,' he whined. 'Come now, sir. That's a shockin' thing to say. To a gentleman like you five 'undred's a mere nothin'. Nothin'. You ain't surely goin' to make a difficulty about a trifle like that?'

'You needn't think you're going to get it from me,' Thwaite said firmly, 'And I'll tell you why. I haven't got it. A small sum I could manage, but not five hundred. You'll never see it in this world.'

Dunn smiled evilly. This was the stage that he really enjoyed.

'Five 'undred, Mr Thwaite,' he murmured. 'You wouldn't cheat a poor man out of his bit of money?'

Thwaite looked at him steadily. 'Don't you be a fool,' he advised. 'I've paid you something like three thousand in the last five years and I'm about fed up. Don't push me too far.'

Dunn's face essayed the expression of injured innocence. 'Too far, Mr Thwaite? I wouldn't put you about, not for the world. I would never have mentioned this trifle if I didn't know you could oblige with ease. Sir, you 'urt my feelin's.'

'I could oblige, could I? Then since you know so much, just tell me how.'

Dunn grinned maliciously. 'I wouldn't have presumed to suggest it, Mr Thwaite, but when you ask my opinion it's another thing. Since you ask me, sir, what about postponin' the Sirius? The Austin is still a good car. Many a man would give his ears for a five-year-old Austin.'

Thwaite swore. 'How the hell do you know about that?' he growled.

'Nothin' in it,' Dunn returned smoothly. 'Everyone knows that Mrs Thwaite 'as been tryin' out the new saloon an' it's not 'ard to guess why.'

It was then that Thwaite finally decided to carry out the plan. He pretended to think, then shifted impatiently in his chair.

'Well,' he said, 'we won't discuss it here. I'll do what I can. Come up tomorrow night and we'll go into it.' The following night Mrs Thwaite was going on a visit to town. 'And by the way,' he added, 'bring those quotations of Maxwell's also. No harm to have a reason for your call.'

So far, so good. Thwaite could see that Dunn suspected nothing. Of course, there was no reason why he should. It was not the first time he had been to Thwaite's house on a similar mission.

Next evening Thwaite made the few simple preparations necessary. He had already put notes for fifty pounds in his pocket and now he made sure that his bankbook, posted to date, was in his safe. Next he wrote a letter to his stockbroker, placed the carbon copy in his file and burned the original. Then he poured away the whisky in the decanter until only two moderate glasses remained, and into this he put half of one of his sleeping powders. He saw that an unopened bottle of whisky, a siphon, plain water and glasses were available. In the right outside pocket of his overcoat, hanging in the passage outside his study door, he put a hammer and in the left an electric torch. Lastly he put on both the clock and his wristwatch ten minutes. Then he sat down to wait.

It was necessary that he take the utmost care. There could not fail to be suspicion and his scheme must be capable of withstanding police investigation. Thwaite was aware that it was generally believed in the office that Dunn had some kind of hold over him. Things were overlooked in Dunn's case which would not be tolerated from anyone else. But Thwaite could have a good alibi. He would be able to prove that he had never left the house.

The need for action over, Thwaite found that he could scarcely bear the weight of horror that was creeping down over him. Like most people, he had read about murderers and had marvelled at the mistakes murders made to their own undoing. Now, though the crime as yet existed only in his imagination, he understood those mistakes. Under the stress of such emotions a man could not think. He seemed as from a distance to see Dunn before him, alive and well, with not a thought of death in his mind. He seemed to see his own arm rise, to hear the sickening thud of the hammer on the man's skull, to watch the body relax and become motionless. Dunn's dead body! Dead all but the eyes. In Thwaite's imagination the eyes seemed to remain alive, staring at him reproachfully, following him about wherever he went. He shuddered. Heavens! If he did this thing would he ever know peace again?

He took out his flask, poured out a stiff tot and gulped it down almost neat. Immediately things once again took on their normal perspective. He had let his nerves run away with him. It was not his way to funk things and he was not going to funk this one. A little courage, a nasty ten minutes and then – safety, release from his present troubles, happiness in his home, assurance for the future! When half an hour later there came a ring at the door and Dunn was shown in, Thwaite was his own man again.

For the benefit of the servant he greeted his visitor cordially. 'It's those Maxwell quotations, I suppose? We'll do them at once.' Then the door closed, he went on: 'Get them out, Dunn, and I'll initial them. No use in taking half a precaution. You came here to get them dealt with and we'll deal with them.'

They settled down to work, as if in Thwaite's room in the works. Fifteen minutes later the business was completed and Dunn pushed the papers back into his pocket. Thwaite leaned back in his chair.

'Now about the other matter,' he said slowly, while Dunn's eyes gleamed avariciously. 'By the way,' Thwaite rose to his feet as if for something he had forgotten, 'have a drink? No use in quarrelling even though we've got unpleasant business to do.'

Suspicion fought with desire in the man's shifty eyes. 'I'll not mind anything tonight,' he quavered.

'Don't be such an unholy fool,' Thwaite said roughly. 'What are you afraid of? Think I'm going to poison you? Here,' he shoved decanter and glasses across the table. 'Pour out the same for us both.' He dumped down the siphon. 'Add the soda yourself and don't be more of an ass than you can help.'

Desire conquered, as Thwaite knew it would. Thwaite drank his first, then Dunn, his suspicions dispelled by this ocular demonstration, followed suit. The dose was small, a quarter of the normal to each man, but it would fulfil its purpose. On Thwaite, because of its many predecessors, it would have no effect to speak of. Dunn it would make sleepy. Thwaite did not wish him put to sleep; he only wanted him to be stupid and off his guard.

With grim satisfaction Thwaite noted his first fence taken. He had now only to see that no inkling of his purpose penetrated the man's mind. He sat forward and became confidential.

'Now look here, Dunn,' he said in the tone of one man of the world to another, 'there's not a bit of use in your talking about five hundred, pounds. I simply haven't got it and that's all there's to it. I told you that already. All the same I'm anxious to meet you. How would this do?'

He took the roll of notes from his pocket and threw it on the table. Then he went to his file and got the copy of the letter to the stockbroker. Dunn seized the notes then slowly, caressingly, as if taking a pleasure in their mere feel, he began to count.

'Fifty?' He cackled dryly. 'You always will have your little joke.'

'Read the letter,' Thwaite said impatiently. Dunn did so, very deliberately. Then very deliberately he finished his whisky and equally deliberately he spoke.

'A sale of stocks for two 'undred an' fifty? You're very jokey tonight, Mr Thwaite.'

'Three hundred, Dunn! Three hundred noted pounds. Six times that roll of notes. Think of it, man! And I don't say,' Thwaite added, 'that it need necessarily be the last. Don't be a fool, Dunn. Take three thousand to go on with and be thankful.'

Dunn slowly smiled his evil smile.

'Five 'undred, Mr Thwaite,' he repeated. 'My son: I mentioned that – '

'Thwaite sprang to his feet and began to pace the room. 'But confound it all, man, haven't I told you I can't do it? Damn it, do you not believe me? Look here.' He pulled out his keys, and going to the built-in safe in the corner of the room, unlocked it, swung the heavy door back, took out his bankbook and slapped it down dramatically on the table. 'Look for yourself. It's posted to this very afternoon.'

Again Dunn cackled thinly. 'A book, Mr Thwaite? You surprise me, sir. Surely a man of your skill with books wouldn't ask a friend like me to believe in a book?'

Thwaite felt a slight relief. The old fool was making his task easier for him. He ignored the gibe.

'Well, I've made you an offer,' he said. 'Fifty pounds now and two hundred and fifty more as soon as my stockbrokers can realize. Take it or leave it. But I tell you seriously that if you don't take it you'll get nothing. I'm at the end of my tether. I'm going to have done with all this.'

'An' may I ask 'ow?'

'You may. I'm going to let you put in your information. It's five years old and I've served the firm well since then. I've saved them a good deal more than that thousand. I'll sell this house and pay the money back with interest. I'll take my medicine, it won't be very much under the circumstances, and then I'll go abroad under a new name and start fresh.'

'Your wife, sir?'

Thwaite swung round. 'Damn you, it's none of your business,' he said angrily. Then more calmly, 'My wife will leave the country first, if you want to know. She'll be waiting for me under the new name when I get out; you'll not know where. She'll wait for me, two or three years; it can't be more. That's what'll happen. You can take your three hundred; I'll make it three hundred a year. Or you can do the other.'

Dunn sat staring at him, rather stupidly. The drug was acting already. Thwaite got a momentary panic that he had given him too much.

'Well,' he said sharply, glancing at the clock. Time was nearly up. 'What about it? Will you take it or leave it?'

'Five 'undred,' Dunn persisted in a slightly thick voice. 'Five 'undred I want. Not a penny less.'

'Right,' Thwaite returned promptly. 'That settles it. Now you can go and do your worst. I've done with you.'

Dunn gazed at him vacantly. Then he leered. 'No darned fear, you 'aven't, Mr Thwaite,' he muttered tipsily. 'Not you. Not such a fool, you ain't. Come, pay up.' He slowly held out a shaking hand. 'Five 'un'red.'

Thwaite glanced at him in real anxiety. 'Not feeling well, Dunn? Have a drop more whisky?' Without waiting for a reply he opened the fresh bottle and poured out a further tot. The clerk sipped it and it seemed to pull him together.

'Strange that, Mr Thwaite,' he remarked. 'I did feel a bit giddy for a time. But I'm better now. Indigestion, I expect.'

'I dare say. Well, if you're going on this train it's time you started. Sleep on this business and let me know your decision tomorrow. Take the fifty in any case.'

The man demurred, but he could not resist the notes and slowly put them in his pocket. Then he looked at his watch and from it to the clock.

'Your clock's fast,' he declared. 'There's ten minutes yet.'

'Fast, is it?' Thwaite returned. 'I don't think so.' He looked at his own wristwatch. 'No, you must be slow. See here.'

Dunn seemed a trifle bemused. He stood up, swaying slightly. Thwaite congratulated himself. It was exactly the condition he had hoped for.

'Look here,' he said, 'you're not quite fit yet. I'll see you to the station. Wait till I get my coat.'

Now that the moment was upon him, Thwaite felt cool and efficient, master of himself and of the situation. He put on his coat, feeling the hammer in the pocket.

'Come along,' he said. 'We'll go out this way. Give me your arm.'

The study was entered from a passage leading from the main hall to a side door into the garden. This door Thwaite now opened, and, when they had passed through, drew it noiselessly to behind him. Presently he would return, let himself in as noiselessly, alter the clock and his watch, make a noisy passage to the hall door, bid someone a cordial good night, and slam the door. At once he would ring, on the pretext that he was working late and wanted more coffee, and when the servant came he would draw her attention to the hour in explaining when to bring it. This would establish, first, that he, Thwaite, had not left the house, and second, that his victim had gone at the proper time to catch his train. These two admitted, his innocence would follow as a matter of course.

It was a fine night, but intensely dark. As they left the house a goods train clanked slowly by. Thwaite almost exulted. His ally! There were plenty of them at this hour. It was on one of them he was counting to blot out his crime. A blow on the head with the hammer; through the man's hat there would be no blood; then it would just be necessary to lay the body on the rails clear of the level crossing and the train would do the rest. There would be a few anxious minutes, then – safety!

Slowly the two men passed on, arm in arm. Now they were in the blackness of the shrubbery. Thwaite knew every step. He had brought the torch only in case of emergency. A breeze met them, faint but chill. It moaned dismally among the pines. Somewhere in the distance a dog barked. There was a little movement in the shrubs; a rabbit perhaps, or a cat. Thwaite's heart began to pump as he steered his unconscious victim towards his dreadful goal. Now they were going down the little sidewalk to the gate. Now they were at the gate, were passing through, were in the lane. Not twenty yards away was the crossing.

It seemed to Thwaite that he had lost his personality as they walked that twenty yards. From a distance he, the real Thwaite, watched this automaton which bore his shape. His brain was numb. Something had to be done by this automaton, something nasty, and with detached interest he watched its performance. They reached the crossing and halted at the wicket. Save for the faint moan of the wind and the rumble of a car on the road all was still. Thwaite grasped the hammer. The moment was upon him.

Then he gave a sudden gasp as a thought flashed devastatingly into his mind. It hit him like a physical blow. He could not do it! He had made a mistake. He had given himself away. For that night at least Dunn was as safe as if he were surrounded by a legion of angels with flaming swords.

His keys! He had left them in the safe. Without them he could not get back into the house. He would have to ring. And if he had been out, no one would believe he had not gone at least as far as the crossing. It was too close to the house. Thwaite leaned against the wicket, grimly remembering his cocksure superiority as he had marvelled at the mistakes of murderers.

Then a rush of relief, almost painful in its intensity, swept over him. What if he had not remembered? Another minute and he would now be a murderer himself, fleeing from justice. The rope would be as good as about his neck. Nothing could have saved him.

The sudden revulsion of feeling unnerved him. For the moment he felt he could stand no more of Dunn. Unsteadily he murmured a good night and a safe home. Turning, he staggered back along the lane.

For ten minutes he paced up and down till he felt his manner had become normal. Then he rang at his door.

'Thank you, Jane,' he said automatically. He still felt in a dream. 'I went to see Mr Dunn over the crossing and forgot my keys.'

His relief at his escape had been instantaneous. Now to his surprise he found another and a deeper relief growing up within him. He was not a murderer! Now he began to see in its true proportions the hideousness of the crime. He felt that his vision had been the truth. If he had done what he intended he would never have got rid of Dunn's eyes. Peace, safety, happiness, assurance? He would never have known one of them! He would have changed his present thraldom for a slavery ten times as severe.

Light-heartedly and thankfully he went to bed. Light-heartedly and thankfully he got up next morning. He would be done with the whole horrid nightmare. That very day he would make a clean breast to the manager, take his medicine and know peace once again.

And then at breakfast the blow fell. Jane, her eyes starting from her head, burst into the room.

'Have you heard the news, sir?' she cried. 'The milkman has just told me. Mr Dunn was killed last night; run over at the crossing! The platelayers found him this morning, terribly cut up!'

Thwaite slowly turned a dead white. *What* had he told the girl last night? Already she was staring at him curiously. What could she be thinking?

With a superhuman effort he pulled himself together. 'Bless my soul!' he exclaimed in shocked accents as he rose from the table. 'Dunn killed! Good Heavens, Jane, how terrible! I'll go down.'

He went down. Already the body had been removed to an adjoining platelayers' hut and the police were in charge. The sergeant saluted as Thwaite appeared.

'Sad affair this, Mr Thwaite,' he said cheerily. 'You knew the old gentleman, didn't you, sir?'

'Knew him?' Thwaite returned. 'Of course I knew him. He worked in my own office. Why, he was with me last night; going into some business. It must have been when he was leaving me that this happened. Awful! It's given me quite a shock.'

'Bound to,' the cheery sergeant sympathized. 'But, Lord, sir, accidents will happen.'

'I know, sergeant, but it's upset me, for I feel a bit responsible about it. He had had a drop too much. I offered him a very moderate drink, but he was evidently not accustomed to it. Of course, it only affected him slightly. All the same I thought it wise to come out to see him safely to the station.'

The sergeant's expression altered. 'Oh, you came out with him, did you? And did you see him to the station?'

'No. The cold air seemed to make him all right. I turned before we reached the crossing.'

Was that the sergeant's ordinary look, or was he – already?

They came that day to make inquiries. They saw him at the office; presumably they saw the servants also. Thwaite told the truth; that he had gone as far as the wicket and then returned home. They took notes and went away.

Next day they came again.

At the trial the defence made much of the fact that Thwaite had gone openly to the crossing; he had not attempted to hide his action either from the servant or the police. But the defence could not explain the sleeping draught found in the dregs of the decanter and in the stomach of the deceased, nor the fact that the study clock had gone ten minutes fast since dinnertime, when Jane had noticed that it was correct. Nor could they hide the significance of a closely written sheet about ledger entries which was found in a sealed envelope in Dunn's lodgings. Nor yet of certain sums which on certain dates had vanished from Thwaite's bank account, and of similar sums which a few days later had appeared in Dunn's. Finally the defence could offer no convincing explanation of two facts: the first, ascertained from dark stains on a certain engine, that the tragedy had taken place seven minutes before Thwaite returned to his house; the second, that the kitchen hammer, bearing Thwaite's fingerprints, should be in the pocket of the old coat he wore that night.

On the last dreadful morning Thwaite told the chaplain the exact truth. Then he showed the courage which was expected from him.

EAST WIND

Inspector Joseph French of the CID had handled in his time a great diversity of cases. Of these, some were remarkable for their dramatic setting, some for the terrible nature of the crimes revealed, and some for the brilliant logical analysis by which the Inspector reached his result. The case which had its beginning on the famous 10.30 a.m. Cornish Riviera Limited Express belonged to none of these categories. In it French was shown, not as the abstract reasoner triumphantly reaching the solution of some baffling problem, but as the practical man of affairs, the organizer using with skill and promptitude the great machine of the British police force.

It was towards the end of May and French had been working for several weeks on an intricate case of forgery in South London. He was tired of Town and longed to get out of it. When therefore it became necessary for him to interview an old lag who was doing a stretch at Princetown, he was delighted. A breath of the air of Dartmoor would come as a pleasant change from the drab and sordid Lambeth streets.

It was with pleasurable anticipation that he drove to Paddington and took his seat in the train. He had a good deal of work to do before he reached the prison, and as soon as the express settled down into its stride, he got out his papers and began. For some hours he read and noted, then with a sigh of relief he bundled the documents back into his bag and turned his attention to the scenery.

They had just passed Exeter and were running down the river opposite Exmouth. The previous night had been wet, but now the sky had cleared and the sun was shining. Everything had been washed by the rain and looked fresh and springlike. The sea, when they reached it, was calm and vividly blue and contrasted strikingly with the red cliffs and pillars of Dawlish and Teignmouth.

They turned up the estuary of the Teign and ran through Newton Abbott. From here to Plymouth French thought the country less interesting and he turned to a novel which he had thrust into his bag. For a few minutes he read, then he heard a whistle and the brakes began to grind on the wheels.

There was no halt scheduled hereabouts, the train running without a stop from London to Plymouth. Repairing the line or blocked by some other train, French thought. Since he had done that job on the Southern near Whitness French rather fancied himself as a railway expert.

The speed decreased and presently they stopped at a small station: Greenbridge, he saw the name was. With a slight feeling of displeasure he was about to apply himself again to his book when he heard a faint report, and another, and another.

Three distant fog signals, he supposed, and as he knew this was an emergency danger signal, he lowered the window and looked out. He was at the platform side and down the platform he saw a sight which brought him to his feet in the twinkling of an eye.

A hold-up was in progress. Some four carriages down the train a door was open and opposite it stood a man, a big stout fellow in grey with a white mask on his face and a pistol in his raised hand. With it he covered the passengers, none of whom was to be seen, but the guard had alighted and was, standing opposite his van, his arms raised above his head.

As French reached the platform two men stepped out of the compartment with the open door. One, medium-sized and dressed in a fawn coat and hat, was also wearing a mask and brandishing a pistol. The other, of about the same height, was without arms or mask, and even at that distance French could sense an eager haste in his movements. The three, the two armed men and the eager one, ran quickly out of the station and immediately the sound of a rapidly accelerating car came from the road.

French dashed to the exit, but the vehicle had disappeared before he reached it. Then he ran back to the compartment from which the men had descended, and which was now surrounded by an excited crowd of passengers. French pushed his way to the front.

In the compartment lay two men in the uniform of prison warders. One was obviously dead, shot through the forehead; the other was hunched up in a corner, apparently unconscious, but with no visible injury.

'I'm a police officer from Scotland Yard,' French shouted. 'I'll take charge here.' He pointed to a couple of the passengers who were crowding round. 'Will you gentlemen search the train quickly for a doctor. You others, close the compartment and let no one in except to attend to the man in the corner. Where is there a telephone, guard?'

The moment French had seen the warders' uniforms, he knew what had taken place. Though it was not his business, he happened to be aware that a prisoner was being conveyed to Dartmoor by the train. He was a man named

94

Jeremy Sandes, and French was interested in him because he was one of his own captures.

The crime for which Sandes had been taken was the theft of Lady Ormsby-Keats' jewels from her country house of Dutton Manor, situated about a mile from Epsom. With forged testimonials he had got a job as footman. This gave him his opportunity. It was suspected that Sandes was only one of a gang and that before capture he had managed to pass on his takings to his accomplices, though neither of these assumptions could be proved. At all events not a single pennyworth of the £17,000 odd of jewellery he had stolen had been recovered.

French's inspiring example galvanized the passengers into activity. A doctor was speedily found, and while he was attending to the warder, French and the guard and some of the passengers ran towards the station buildings. The station was little more than a halt, but there was a general waiting-room and a tiny ticket office. Of these, the office was locked. French rattled at the door. 'Anybody there?' he shouted.

For answer, a dismal groan came from within. French and the guard threw themselves on the door, but it was strongly made and resisted their efforts.

'The seat,' French pointed.

On the platform was a heavy wooden seat. Willing hands quickly raised it, and using it as a battering ram, swung it back and brought its end crashing against the door. With the tearing sound of splintering wood the keeper gave way and the door swung open.

In the little office was a single chair and on the chair sat a man in porter's uniform. He was securely gagged with a cloth and bound to the chair with a rope. A few seconds only sufficed to release him. Beyond the possibility of apoplexy from suppressed fury, he seemed none the worse for his experience.

'The big man came in with a mask on his face,' he spluttered indignantly, 'and before I could move I found myself looking into the wrong end of a gun. Then the second man came in and I was tied up before you could say knife.'

'Anyone else about the station?' French asked sharply.

'Yes, there's the signalman. They must have tied him up too, else they couldn't have stopped the train.'

The signal-box was at the end of the platform to the rear and the little party hurried down. It was as the porter suggested. The signalman was seated on a stool, bound and gagged, but uninjured.

He had, he said, been sitting in his box, when he noticed two men pacing the other end of the platform, as if measuring. They disappeared, then a few minutes later they suddenly rushed up the box steps and covered him with their guns. He could do nothing and was at once gagged and bound. He had already accepted the express and pulled off the signals, and the men at once threw the latter to danger. They waited till the departure came through for the express, acknowledged the signal correctly, then they cut the block and telephone wires. When the train appeared and was slowing down they pulled off the home signal, leaving the distant and starter at danger. This was correct railway practice and showed that they knew what they were doing. The result was that the train pulled up at the platform. When they lowered the home signal they hurried down to the platform, and were ostensibly reading a time bill with their backs to the line when the train came in. They evidently knew where the prisoner was, for they had been waiting opposite his compartment and opened its door without hesitation.

French heard the story in the briefest outline and then asked for a description of the men. But he could get nothing of value. Between the speed with which everything had happened and the masks which had been worn, only a blurred picture of their assailants had been left in the railwaymen's minds.

He ran back to the train, and holding up his hand for silence, asked if anyone had noticed any peculiarity about the men by which they might be recognized. For a moment there was no reply, then a lady in the compartment adjoining that of the tragedy came forward.

She had been in the window and had had plenty of time to observe the big man who had kept guard on the platform. She could not of course see his face, but she was able to describe his clothes. These were quite ordinary except for one point. On the toe of his rather elegant black shoe were three small spots of mud forming the angles of a tiny equilateral triangle.

This was the only clue French could get, but it was of an entirely satisfactory nature. If the big man did not notice the marks and rub them off, they might well lead to his undoing.

French turned again to the railwaymen asking urgently where was the nearest telephone. Their wires in the signal-box being cut, the porter advised application to Farmer Goodbody, who lived three hundred yards up the road. It would be quicker, he said, than travelling on by the train to the next station.

In three minutes French was knocking at the farmer's door and in another two he was speaking to the superintendent in Exeter. He had been extremely quick in his inquiries and not more than ten minutes had elapsed since the crime. The fugitives could not have gone more than seven or eight miles at the most and prompt action should enable a police ring to be thrown round the area before they could get clear. French however asked that they should not be arrested, but only shadowed.

He was able to supply very fair descriptions of the trio. About the prisoner, Jeremy Sandes, he could give complete information. He had worked at his description so often that he remembered it in detail. As to the others, he knew their height and build, and there was that priceless point about the three spots of mud.

The information was passed to Exeter, Plymouth, Okehampton and other centres, as well as to the Yard. Arrangements were made about the bodies of the dead warders and then French rang up the nearest village for a car and was driven into Newton Abbott. There he was fortunate enough to find a train just about to start for Exeter. Forty minutes later he reached police headquarters in that city. Superintendent Hambrook was an old friend and received him with effusion.

'We've done what you said, Inspector,' he went on. 'As far as we have men to do it, all roads have been blocked in a circle from here through Crediton, Okehampton, Tavistock and Plymouth, and we are having the Exmouth ferry and all ports in the area watched. That circle is about twenty to twenty-five miles radius as the crow flies and it would take the parties thirty or forty minutes to reach it. With luck we'll get them. But, French, are you sure you're right in not arresting them? If you lose them now they mayn't be easy to get again.'

'I know, super, but I think it's worth the risk. What do you suppose this escape was organized for?'

Hambrook closed his right eye. 'The swag?' he suggested.

French nodded. 'That's it. They'd never have committed murder just to help their pal. This Sandes has hidden the stuff and the others were left. Now they're going to make him fork up.'

'And you want to let him find it?'

'He's the only one who can.'

'It's an idea,' the super admitted doubtfully. 'But I don't know. If it were my case I think I'd go for the bird in the hand.'

French's reply was interrupted by a strident ring on the super's telephone bell. Hambrook picked up the receiver, handing a second to French.

'Constable Cunningham speaking from the London by-pass, Exeter. I think we've identified the big man and the prisoner, Sandes. They're driving towards London in a Daimler limousine Number AZQ 9999. If we're right, they've changed their clothes. The big man is wearing a dark coat and hat, but when we had him out we saw the three spots of mud on his left toe. The driver answers the description of Sandes, though his face has been darkened and he's wearing chauffeur's uniform. The big man gave the name Mr Oliver Hawke, diamond merchant, of 767B Hatton Garden and St Austell's, Brabfield Road, Hampstead. They stopped at once and were quite civil. They said they were coming from the 'Burlington Hotel' in Plymouth and going home. We let them go and Constable Emerson is following them on the motorbike. The tyres are newish Dunlops.'

French was highly delighted. 'If they're being civil and answering questions it means they've fixed up an alibi and feel safe about it.' He rubbed his hands. 'A diamond merchant! The best fence in the world!'

Hambrook agreed and French went on. 'I bet you anything you like Hawke's going home as he says. If so, we'll get him there, and Sandes too. Ring up ahead, will you, super? If he's making for Town we'll call off the pursuit.'

While Hambrook was telephoning French had been studying a timetable. 'There's an express at 5.42,' he said. 'If they go towards London I'll take it. I confess I'd like to be in Hampstead to see them arrive. Just get the Plymouth men to look up that hotel, will you, super?'

The 'Burlington' reported that Mr Hawke and his chauffeur had stayed there for the past two nights and had left for London that day about noon. They had taken lunch with them and said they would eat it in the car *en route*.

'There's the alibi emerging already,' French declared. 'Why did they take so long between Plymouth and Exeter? Because they stopped for lunch. Why were they not seen at any hotel? Because they took it in the car. Quite. Now the Yard, like a good fellow.'

To headquarters French reported what had happened, asking if a Mr Hawke lived and moved and had his being at the address given, and if so, what was this gentleman like in appearance? In a short time there was a reply which showed that the man in the car had given his real name.

French rose. 'I'll just get that train if I look slippy,' he said. 'Well, super, glad to have seen you again. If your people come on that other ruffian, I'd shadow him also. We think there's still another of them in the gang and we may as well have a shot for the lot.'

As French sat thinking over the affair in the up express he saw that there definitely must have been another confederate. The two men at Greenbridge had known in which compartment the prisoner was travelling. Now it was impossible that they could have evolved this information out of their own inner consciousness. It must therefore have been sent to them, and there was only one way in which it could have been obtained. Someone had watched the man and his escort entraining at Paddington. French wondered could he trace a trunk call or a telegram from Paddington shortly after 10.30 that morning.

At Taunton, their first stop, French sent wires in veiled language to the Yard and the Exeter super, asking the former to find out if such a message had been sent, and the latter if Hawke had called anywhere to receive it. Then feeling he had done his duty by the case for the moment, he went to the dining car for a long delayed meal.

At nine o'clock French stepped down on to the platform at Paddington and fifteen minutes later was at the Yard. There he found his colleague Inspector Tanner waiting for him.

'I've been handling this stuff of yours,' said Tanner. 'Your friends are coming up nicely. They were seen passing through Chard, Shaftesbury, Salisbury, Andover and Basingstoke. They dined at Basingstoke and left there half an hour ago. They should be in Hampstead between ten and eleven. We'll go out and see them arrive.'

'Get anything about Hawke's business?'

'Small one-man show. Doesn't seem to be much going on. Yet Hawke must be well-to-do, judging by the house he lives in. I went to the office to ask for him. The clerk made no bones about it. Mr Hawke was down at Plymouth on business, but was coming up today and would be available tomorrow.'

'I thought that part of it would be all right.'

'What about arresting him now, French?' Tanner went on earnestly. 'If we find him in the company of Sandes we have him; he can't put any kind of defence. Once we let them separate we'll find the case a darned sight harder to prove.'

'And what about the swag?' French returned. 'No, we'll take the risk. And there's another point you've missed. As you know, we believe there are four men in the gang. Now we want them all. If we arrest Hawke and Sandes tonight, we may lose the other two. No, let's watch them: we may get the lot. By the way, did you find out anything about that message from Paddington?'

'Yes, we've got something there.' Tanner drew a scrap of paper from his pocket. With eagerness French read it. 'Quotation required Exodus chapter six verse four.' 'It was sent at 10.40 from the telegraph office at Paddington.' Tanner went on, 'to "Anderton, Post Restante, Plymouth." It was called for at 11.45 by a man resembling Hawke. Does that give you any light?'

French nodded delightedly. 'I should just think it does!' he declared with enthusiasm. 'You see it, of course? The sixth carriage from the engine and the fourth compartment. That's what the men were measuring on the platform at Greenbridge. If those post-office people in Plymouth can swear to Hawke, that'll come in handy.'

'Pretty sure to, I should think.' Tanner glanced anxiously at the clock. 'Your friends should have been past Blackwater before now. It's only fifteen miles from Basingstoke and they've left nearly forty minutes.' He picked up his telephone and asked for Blackwater. 'No sign,' he said presently. 'I don't like this, French. Have they turned aside?'

French was already examining a large-scale road map.

'Reading or Farnham are the obvious, places north and south,' he answered, 'but there are endless roads in between. Give a general call over that area, Tanner.'

Tanner did so as quickly as he could and they settled down to wait. As the minutes passed French became more anxious than he cared to show. Had he overreached himself? If so, and if these two got away, it would be a pretty serious thing for him. Yet, he told himself, they *couldn't* get away.

Once again the telephone bell rang. 'Blackwater at last,' said Tanner with relief. Then his expression changed. 'Oh, you have? Good man, sergeant! Splendid! I'll wait for his report.' He rang off.

'Blackwater reports that when they didn't turn up he sent a man out on a motorbike to look for them and he's found them parked up a side road near Basingstoke. He's watching them and will keep us advised what happens.'

'What's that for on earth?' French queried.

Tanner shook his head and once more they settled down to wait. And wait they did, endlessly and with growing mystification. Twice at intervals of an hour the constable rang up on an accommodating householder's telephone to say that the men were still sitting in the stationary car, but the third message, when it came at half past twelve, showed that the halt was over.

'Speaking from Farnham,' the constable reported. 'About twelve they started and ran here and have gone on towards Guildford. I've asked the Guildford men to have a look out and ring you.'

'Guildford!' French exclaimed anxiously. 'What in Hades are they going there for?' He glanced at Tanner. On his face was imprinted the same anxiety.

Once again the bell rang. 'They've been seen,' Tanner reported. 'They passed through Guildford four minutes ago in the Leatherhead direction. The Guildford men have already rung up Leatherhead.'

Suddenly French started. Leatherhead! Leatherhead was near Epsom. Not more than three or four miles between them. With a rising excitement he wondered if he could guess their destination.

In a moment his mind was made up. He would stake everything on this idea of his. He spoke quickly to Tanner.

Tanner swore. 'You can go at once,' he answered with equal speed. 'The cars are waiting to go to Hampstead. I'll be here if you want anything.'

A moment later French was racing down the corridor to the courtyard. There, with Sergeant Carter and a number of plain-clothes men, were two police cars.

'Come on, men,' French shouted. 'Tumble in. Hard as you can lick to Epsom.' Ten seconds later the cars glided out on to the Embankment and turned south over Westminster Bridge.

French had done many a race by car, but seldom had he made such going as on the present occasion. Traffic in the streets was at a low ebb and they took full advantage of it. They gave way to nothing, slinging across the fronts of trams and causing other motorists to jam on their brakes and complain to the nearest policeman. Twice disaster was avoided by a hair's-breadth, and again and again only profound skill saved a spill. So, leaving behind them a trail of indignant and exasperated drivers, they rushed on through the streets.

Presently they left Town behind them and still further increased their speed. The edge of the road became a quivering line in the light of their headlamps and their tyres roared on the asphalt surface. The needles of their speedometers rose and rose till for one brief moment on a down-grade straight they touched 65. Their horns were seldom silent, and more than once as they took curves French thanked his stars the road was not greasy.

At Epsom they swung quickly in to the police station. A sergeant was waiting on the footpath.

'Your car went through seven minutes ago,' he said quickly: 'towards Burgh Heath.'

This news practically confirmed French's idea. Dutton Manor lay about a mile out along the Burgh Heath road.

'Good,' he cried with a feeling of relief. 'After it, drivers.'

Once again their tyres roared over the smooth road. A mile slipped away in a few seconds.

'Steady,' said French presently. 'Stop before you get to that corner.'

Round the corner was a straight upon which the Manor front and back drives debouched. As the cars came to a stand French leaped out and ran forward with his torch, followed by his men. They passed round the corner and reached the straight. No car lights were visible ahead.

This, however, was scarcely to be expected and they raced on, keeping for the sake of silence along the grass verge. Presently they came to the front entrance.

With his torch held vertically so as not to betray their presence, French made a hurried examination of the drive. It was surfaced with gravel and the recent rain had softened it. He could have sworn that no car had passed over it recently. Calling softly to his followers, he hurried on along the road.

From his investigation at the time of the robbery French knew every inch of the little domain. The back drive was a hundred yards farther along the road and this was his new objective.

When he shone his torch on the ground at its entrance he gave a grunt of satisfaction. There entering the drive were fresh tyre marks, fairly new Dunlops. Good for the Exeter constable's observation!

More cautiously they hurried up the drive, the men moving with speed and silence. There was no moon, but the stars gave a certain light. A wind had been blowing earlier, but it had died down and now everything was still. Suddenly French thought he heard a voice. A touch passed down the line and all instantly became rigid.

Yes, people were moving a short distance ahead and speaking in low tones. French crept stealthily forward.

'...stopped us at Exeter,' he heard a man say in low tones, 'but they didn't suspect anything and we passed through all right. How did you manage, Taylor?'

'I garaged the car at Newton Abbott and came by train,' returned another voice. 'I reached Paddington at 6.55, got your 'phone from a Basingstoke, picked up Gould and came on here. What's it all about, Hawke?'

'The swag. Sandes had hidden it here. I thought we ought all to be here in case – '

The speaker must have turned away, for French lost the remainder of the sentence. Crouching back into the hedge, he could now see four figures moving like shadows in front of him. They were entering the drive from a field, obviously after hiding their car. As they turned towards the house, French and his men dropped in behind.

To say that French was delighted would convey no impression of his state of mind. From the first he had felt that only hope of recovery of the swag could account for the rescue of Sandes. Now his ideas and his actions had been abundantly justified. A little more patience and a little more care and both men and jewels would be his! Something more than a triumph, this! Out of what had seemed defeat he would snatch an overwhelming victory!

The two parties were now silently creeping up the drive with a hundred feet or more between them. Surely, French thought, the quarry would not go near the yard, where there were dogs and where the chauffeur slept? No, they were turning aside. They left the drive through a small gate which led to the side of the house, and began to work forward over grass sward containing flowerbeds and a fountain. Here in the open French's little band had to drop back to avoid being seen, but on reaching some clumps of shrubs they closed up again.

French was growing more and more surprised. It was beginning to look as if the others were meditating an attack on the house itself. They were certainly moving on to the very walls. Then suddenly French saw where they were going. Just in front of them was a loggia. He knew it well. It was a biggish area, some fifty feet by twenty, and was roofed and bounded by the house on two sides, but, save for pillars, was open on the third and fourth. On it gave a passage from the main hall, as well as French windows from the principal reception-room, while a short flight of stone steps led down to the terrace. These steps were in the centre of the longer open side, which faced south-west. The short open side faced south-east. These sides were edged with a stone balustrade and every few feet were pedestals bearing large stone vases, each containing a laurustinus.

French's heart beat more rapidly. The end, whatever it might be, was upon them. He wondered if he were about to witness housebreaking. The French windows would be just the place to try, but as he knew them to be fitted with burglar alarms, he did not think the attempt would succeed. Well, if Hawke & Co. gave back, believing they had aroused the household, he and his men would be ready for them.

Slowly and silently the four men crept up the stone steps to the loggia, and as they disappeared within, French and his followers slipped up against the wall at each side of the steps. The floor was some four feet high, and standing on the grass, the watchers could see in between the stone balusters. Contrary to French's expectation the quarry did not approach the French windows. Instead they moved like shadows over to the north-east corner, where the shorter open side joined the wall of the house. French, slipping round the corner, crept along the outside of that short side till he came opposite where they had congregated. They had turned a torch on the floor, which gave a faint light in all directions.

'All quiet.' The whisper came from the man who had been referred to as Hawke. 'Now, Sandes.'

A shadow detached itself from the group and came forward towards French, who shrank down beneath the floor-level. ' 'Ere in this 'ere vase,' he heard in a Cockney whisper. 'It were the nearest place outside the 'ouse I could find and because of the east wind no one sits in this 'ere corner.'

Slowly French raised his head. With a thrill of excitement which he would have died rather than admit, he watched the man put his hand over the edge of the vase and feel about. Then the man gave a sudden grunt, snatched the torch from Hawke, and shone it into the basin. Finally, throwing all caution to the winds, he began to grope wildly. The others had closed in around him.

'Well,' said Hawke, and there was a sharp tenseness in his voice. 'Where is it?'

From Sandes there came a sort of dreadful strangled cry. Then as if reckless from fury and disappointment he swore a lurid oath 'It's not there!' he cried aloud. 'It's gone! Someone 'as taken it!'

'Silence you fool,' Hawke hissed. He snatched the torch from Sandes and gazed into the vase. 'You – liar!' he went on, and his voice, low as it was, cut like a knife. 'The soil where you haven't disturbed it hasn't been moved for months! It's grown green scum. See, you others.'

The other two men looked and cursed in low tones.

'Now, see you,' Hawke went on, still hissing venomously like an angry snake. 'You tell us where that stuff is inside ten seconds or this knife goes into your heart. You thought you'd do us out of our shares so that you could have it all when you got out of quod, and now you think you can put us off with fairy tales! I suspected this and that's why I brought these others.' He raised his hand, which held a long pointed knife. 'You won't escape, Sandes, and we'll all be responsible for your death. Now where is it? I'll give you till I count ten. Hold him, you others.'

French wondered if he should take a hand. He believed Hawke was in earnest and he couldn't stand there and see murder done. Then he realized that Hawke would delay in the hope of learning the truth. And as he himself was quite as anxious as the others to hear what Sandes had to say, he also waited, his heart thumping from the suspense.

'One!' Hawke paused, then went on slowly: 'Two! Three! Hold his mouth, will you!' French saw the little knot bunch together. Hawke raised the knife and began to press the point against the little man's breast. Suddenly the prisoner began to struggle violently. Hawke withdrew the knife.

'We're not bluffing,' he whispered in that voice of steel. 'If we don't get our shares this knife goes into your heart. I've counted to three.' Again he paused. 'Four!' And again. 'Five!' And again. 'Six!' Then came another voice. 'Try him with the knife again, guv'nor,' said the man who had not previously spoken.

'No, no, no!' came in a muffled scream. 'I've told you the truth, I swear I 'ave. I 'id it there.' He swore by all his gods. 'If you kill me I can't tell you no more!'

'Hold him again,' said Hawke inexorably, once more raising the knife.

French felt he couldn't stand this any more. He believed Sandes. He recognized the ring of truth as well as of desperate despairing fear in his voice. The man had, French felt sure, hidden the stuff there in that vase and – someone else had got it and was sitting tight. Perhaps a gardener or one of the servants…He began edging round the wall to the steps.

He had formed his men for the assault and they were able to rush up the steps to take the others by surprise, when there came a terrible scream from above, followed by Hawke's savage voice: 'That's torn it, you – fools! Why couldn't you hold his mouth as I said? We may run for it now! Bring him along!'

Dispensing with any further attempt to preserve silence, the three men dashed across the loggia, dragging the fourth with them. So headlong was their flight that they did not see the waiting constables till they were at the steps. Then arose a terrible outcry. 'The cops!' yelled Hawke with a furious oath. 'Leave Sandes and get away, over the balustrade!' As he shouted he doubled back, fumbling desperately in his pocket. French, flashing out his torch, rushed forward, followed by his men. As Hawke drew a pistol French closed with him.

Now the loggia became a nightmare of whirling bodies, of groans and curses, of thuds and – a couple, of times – of pistol shots. The torches had been knocked down and had gone out and no one could see what he was doing. Everyone clung to whoever he could feel, but he had no idea who he was holding. Three of the policemen found themselves struggling together and it was a couple of minutes before they discovered it and went to their companions' help. Then French touched a torch with his foot and managed to pick it up. With the light the end came quickly. There were eight police to three criminals, for Sandes was too much overcome to take any part in the *mêlée*.

'Take them along to the cars, Carter,' French panted.

Presently, handcuffed, the four men were led off, while French remained behind to assuage the fears of those in the Manor.

★　　★　　★

Next morning French walked up to have a look at the scene of the combat. With Sergeant Carter he stood in the centre of the loggia and looked around.

'Do you see anything interesting?' he said presently, and when the sergeant had failed to give the required reaction, he went on: 'That corner where Sandes said he hid the stuff gets the east wind. You remember he said he chose it because for that reason no one sat there. And yet I notice that the plants there are finer and more healthy than those on the sheltered south side. Does that suggest anything to you? Ah, it does, does it? Then let us see.'

He walked over to the poorest of the plants, which looked indeed as if it had been scorched by wind. In the vase he began to dig with his penknife.

'Ah,' he said in accents of deepest satisfaction. 'What have we here? I think this is Sandes' little lot!'

It was a lucky deduction. In a parcel were the whole of the jewels, and an inquiry from the head gardener showed that only the week before he had changed the vases round, so as to get the poorer shrubs out of the east wind.

At the trial only Hawke and Taylor could be proved guilty of murder, the sending of the telegram not being held to cover compliance with all that had been done at Greenbridge. The first two were executed and the others spent many years in retreat from their normal haunts. In gratitude for French's work Lady Ormsby-Keats contributed £500 to police charities, so for a two-fold reason French felt his efforts had not been wasted.

THE PARCEL

Some twenty years ago Messrs Selwyn & Blount invited six writers of detective fiction 'to commit, upon paper, a murder which they felt to be as perfect in its execution as they could conceive'. I was one of the lucky six and 'The Parcel' was my effort. All were published in *Six Against the Yard*.

But we were not to get off so easily. It was Messrs Sclwyn & Blount's sinister design that Ex-Superintendent Cornish of the CID should 'deal with the crime from the police point of view'. It is by the courtesy of Messrs Selwyn & Blount and the Ex-Superintendent that I am now enabled to reproduce his criticism of 'The Parcel'. For this concession I am most grateful.

FWC

Stewart Haslar's face was grim and his brow dark as he sat at the desk in his study gazing out of the window with unseeing eyes. For he had just taken a dreadful decision. He was going to murder his enemy, Henry Blunt.

For three years he had suffered a crescendo of torment because of Blunt. Now he could stand it no longer. He had reached the end of his tether. Everything that he held dear, everything that made life endurable, was threatened. While Blunt lived he would know neither peace or safety. Blunt must die.

It was when he was turning into the road from the drive of his house one afternoon just three years ago that the blow had fallen. He had got out of his car to close the gate behind him and had met the old man. Something familiar about the long face and the close-set eyes had stirred a chord of memory. In spite of himself he had stared. Blunt had stared too: an insolent leer which changed slowly to a look of amazed recognition. That had been the end of Haslar's peace of mind. But now he was going to get it back. Blunt would trouble him no longer.

It was an old story, that which had given Blunt his power, the story of a happening which Haslar had believed was dead and buried in the past. It went back five and thirty years, back to when he, Haslar, was a youth of twenty and Blunt had just passed his thirty-first birthday.

Five and thirty years ago Haslar's name was John Matthews and he was a junior clerk in the head office of the Scottish Counties Bank in Edinburgh. Henry Blunt was in the same department, but in a more responsible job. Matthews was a good lad, well thought of by his superiors. But Blunt was of a very different type. With charming manners, he was wholly selfish and corrupt.

Owing to a run of bad luck at cards, Blunt's finances were then at a very low ebb. Ruin indeed was staring him in the face. He decided on a desperate remedy. In the bank he was handling money all day. If only he had the help of a junior clerk he believed he saw a way in which he could transfer a large sum to his own pocket. He decided to use Matthews and made overtures of friendship. Matthews was flattered at the notice taken of him by the older man and responded warmly. He did not know that Blunt merely wanted a dupe.

Blunt had weighed up the young fellow's character accurately. He didn't think he would be troubled by moral scruples, but he feared he might refuse his help through fear of consequences. Blunt was taking no risks. He decided to prepare the ground before sowing his seed. With skill he introduced Matthews to his gambling friends and with fair words got him to play. After that matters were simple. In a few weeks Matthews' position was as desperate as his own.

The psychological moment had come. Blunt put up his scheme. There was a chance of being caught, yes, but it was so slight as to be negligible. But without the scheme there would be certain ruin. Which would Matthews choose?

The result was a foregone conclusion. Matthews joined in. The attempt was made. It failed. Matthews was taken red-handed.

At the inquiry Matthews told the truth. But he had not reckoned on the diabolical cunning of Blunt. Blunt had prepared evidence to prove that Matthews and Matthews alone was guilty. He had intended to collar and hide his share of the money before producing the evidence. But events forced his hand. To save himself he had to forgo the profits and make his statement at once.

In the face of the evidence Matthews was found guilty and sentenced to eighteen months' imprisonment. No official suspicion fell on Blunt, but it was privately believed he had been mixed up in the affair. Between the cold shouldering he received in consequence and his debts, Edinburgh grew too hot to hold him. He resigned his position and disappeared.

When Matthews was released he took the name of Haslar and at once shipped before the mast for Australia. It was a hard passage, but it was the making of him. When he reached Sydney he was a man.

For a few years he lived an adventurous life, meeting the ups and downs of fortune with a brave front. Then with borrowed capital he started a small fruit shop. From the first it was a success. He soon paid back what he owed and then put all his profits into the concern. One shop after another was opened, till at last he found himself the owner of a chain of stores, all doing well. For the first time he relaxed and went, so far as he could get the entry, into Melbourne society. There it was that he met his wife Gina, out on a holiday from England. They were married two months later. Gina did not, however, like Australia, and presently at her request he sold his business and returned with her to England, a comparatively wealthy man. She wanted to be near London, and he bought a house in a delightfully secluded position near Oxshott.

Here both of them enjoyed life as they had never done before. Haslar was pleasant and unassuming and soon grew popular with the neighbours. Gina had many friends in Town and rejoined the circles which she had left on her trip to Australia. The couple got on well together and had pleasant little weekend parties at their home. Everything was friendly and pleasant and secure. Haslar had never imagined anything so delightful.

Until Blunt came.

The meeting with Blunt gave Haslar a terrible shock. Instantly he saw that his security, his happiness, the security and happiness of his wife, everything in fact that was precious to him, was at the mercy of this evil-looking old man. Once a whisper of his history became known, his life in this charming English country was done. That he had fully paid for his crime would count not one iota. The righteous people among whom he lived would be defiled if they met a person who had been in prison. Both he and Gina would be cut to their faces. Life would be impossible.

And it would not meet the case to leave Oxshott for some other district, for some other country even. In these days of universal travel their identity could not long remain hidden. No, Blunt had both of them in his hands. If he chose, he could ruin them.

And Blunt was equally well aware of the fact. At that disastrous meeting, as soon as the man realized that the fine little estate from which Haslar had emerged was the latter's own property, Haslar had seen the realization grown in his face; wonder, incredulity, assurance, exultation: it had been easy to follow the thoughts which passed through his mind. And they had soon been put into words. 'Like coming home in my old age, this is,' Blunt had said, adding with an evil leer that he would not have no further troubles, as he knew his old pal would see him comfortable for the rest of his time.

Haslar had acted promptly. 'Get in,' he had said, pointing to the car. 'We can't stand indefinitely on the road. I'll run you wherever you want to go and we'll have a good chat on the way.' Blunt had hesitated as if he would prefer to be taken to the house, but Haslar's determined manner had its effect and he climbed in. By a stroke of extraordinary luck no one had seen the meeting.

What might have been expected then took place. During the drive Blunt made his demand. They were old pals. Haslar had gone up in the world while Blunt had gone down. For the sake of old times Haslar couldn't see his old pal go where he was now heading – to the Embankment seats or the fourpenny doss. Blunt didn't want much. He had no intention of sponging on his friend. A tiny cottage and a few shillings a week for food were all he asked.

Though Blunt had gone all to pieces and seemed suffering from senile decay, he was discreet enough in his conversation. He made no mention of the force which gave his somewhat maundering requests their compulsion. His only reference to it was veiled. 'I hate talking of unpleasant things,' he declared with his evil leer. 'We're good pals, you and I. Let's not mention anything that's disagreeable.'

Haslar indeed was surprised at the man's moderation, though as they talked he realized that the tiny cottage and few shillings a week were rather a figure of speech than an exact description of Blunt's demand. However, what the man asked for could be given him with a negligible outlay. Haslar promised he would see to it.

'But look here, Blunt,' he went on, 'this is an agreement for our mutual benefit. I'll do my part if and as long as you do yours, and no longer. I admit that the information you have is worth something to me and I'm willing to pay for it. I'll get you a small cottage and make you an allowance so that you'll be comfortable on one condition – that you keep my secret. That means more than not telling it. It means that you must do nothing by which people might find it out. You mustn't ever come near Oxshott. If you want to see me, telephone, giving some other name. What name are you going under now?'

'Jamison. I reckon Blunt died in Edinburgh.'

Haslar nodded. 'So did Matthews. I'm now Haslar. Matthews is never to be mentioned. See?'

Blunt, who appeared to be overwhelmed by his good luck, swore by all his gods that he would keep his bargain. Haslar thought he meant it. All the same he rubbed in his point of view.

'I admit, Blunt, that you can injure me if you want to. You spill your story and this place gets too hot for me. I have to go. I don't want to, so I'll pay you as long as you hold your tongue. But talk: and see what else happens. I leave here and go abroad and settle down where I'm not known. My money goes with me and I remain comfortable. But your money stops. You hurt me slightly, but you destroy yourself.'

In the end Haslar gave the man money to take a tiny cottage in a country backwater near Rickmansworth. He made an estimate of what it would cost him to live in reasonable comfort, including the daily visit of a woman to 'do' for him. To this sum Haslar added ten per cent. Handing over the first instalment, he undertook to pay a similar amount on the first Monday of every month. On his part Blunt expressed himself as well satisfied and pledged himself as long as the payment continued never to approach or annoy Haslar.

It was bad, Haslar thought grimly when all this had been arranged, but it was not so bad as it might have been.

II

The arrangement between Haslar and Blunt worked well – for nearly a year. Every first Monday of the month Haslar folded ten £1 notes into a cheap envelope, bought each time specially for the purpose, and at precisely half past one o'clock left a certain prearranged telephone booth in an unobtrusive position in Victoria Station. Blunt on these occasions was always waiting to telephone, and the envelope hidden in the red directory by the one was duly found by the other.

But before the year was up Haslar's fears were realized. Blunt made a fresh demand. One evening he rang up and asked in a surprisingly cultivated voice where they could meet. Haslar fixed a point on the Great North Road and picked the other up in his car.

Blunt was cynically complaisant as he explained his desires. His manner suggested his certainty that he could have what he chose to ask. He was not so comfortable that he had grown bored. No longer faced with the need for work, time hung heavily on his hands. He wanted money to amuse himself. Not much – Haslar need not be alarmed. A very little would satisfy him. All he wished was to be able to go two or three times a week to the pictures, to take an occasional excursion on a bus, and to pay for his glass and stand his treat at the 'Green Goat'.

To Haslar the additional amount was negligible, but he was disturbed by the principle of the thing. He had never before been blackmailed, but all the tales he had read about it stressed the inevitable growth of the demands. What might be insignificant at first swelled eventually to an intolerable burden.

During ten miles of slow driving Haslar considered whether he should not now, at once, make his stand. Then very clearly he saw three things. The first was that he couldn't really make a stand. He could only bluff. If Blunt called his bluff, as he certainly would, he, Haslar, would be done for. He would have to give way. He would be worse off than he was now, for his weakness would have actually been demonstrated.

The second point was that Blunt's demands still remained moderate. In this Haslar could not but consider himself lucky.

The third was that the proposal was really to his, Haslar's, advantage. The more fully occupied was Blunt's time, the less dangerous he would be. Contented, he would think of fewer grievances than if he were bored.

Haslar decided that when he had already gone so far, he would be a fool to fight on so small an issue. But if he were going to give way, he must do it with a good grace. Blunt must not be allowed to suppose there had been any trial of strength. He still further slackened speed and turned to the old man.

'I wasn't hesitating about the money,' he said pleasantly. 'I don't think what you want is unreasonable and I don't mind the small extra. But I was trying to put myself in your place. With all that time on my hands I should fish. What do you think of that? If you'd like it, I'll put up the outfit.'

Blunt was obliged, though always there was that ugly sardonic leer in his eye. He considered himself lucky that his relations with his old pal were so satisfactory. But he was not and never would be a fisherman. If he had the other two or three little things he had asked for, he would be content.

From this time the ten pounds a month became fourteen. The arrangement again worked well, this time for six months. Then Blunt telephoned for another interview. That telephone message was the beginning of Haslar's real trouble. The amount asked for again was small: an extra lump sum of £20 to go on a motor trip to Cornwall. Haslar gave it, but said in half joke, whole earnest, that he was not made of money and that Blunt must not forget it would only pay him to help his friend up to a certain amount. Blunt had replied by asking what was £20 to a man of Haslar's wealth? and had stated in so many words that he was reckoning that to keep his present position would be worth many hundreds a year to his old pal.

Four months later came a further demand: that the fourteen pounds a month should be increased to £20. This time the request took more the form of an ultimatum than a prayer. Moreover Blunt was at less pains to justify it. He simply remarked carelessly that he found he couldn't do on the smaller sum.

At last, Haslar felt, it was time to make a stand. He made it – with the result he might have foreseen, with the result that in his secret mind he had foreseen. Blunt for the first time showed his hand. He swept the other's protestations aside. His demands, he declared, were over-moderate. The secret was worth vastly more than he was getting for it. He was surprised at Haslar being so unreasonable. Instead of asking a beggarly £250 a year he might have had a couple of thousand. And he would have a couple of thousand if there was any more trouble about it. He would have his £20 a month, or would Haslar rather make it £25?

Increasingly Haslar felt his bondage. Not that the payments incommoded him. They had still to mount a long way before he would really feel them; but now fear for the future was growing. Blunt was not exactly an old man. He might live for another twenty years. And if his demands went on increasing – as Haslar believed they were pretty certain to do – how would things end?

The realization of his power now seemed to intoxicate Blunt. His demands grew more frequent and they were made with less regard for Haslar's feelings. Still worse, the old man ceased to show the scrupulous care to keep their meetings secret which he had done at first and which Haslar demanded. No harm had come through this, but it was disconcerting.

Blunt's first large request, not very politely worded, was for a fifty-guinea radio gramophone and a mass of records. The money again didn't much trouble Haslar, though he could no longer say he was not feeling the drain. But he was beginning to see that this state of things could not go on indefinitely. Sooner or later the man would demand something which he could not give, and then what would happen?

After an ineffectual demur, for which he despised himself, Haslar handed over the price of the gramophone. From that moment Blunt's demands increased in geometrical progression. The more he was given, the more he asked. Haslar was now parting with quite a considerable proportion of his income, and he began to envisage either cutting down his own expenses or drawing on his capital. The former he wished to avoid at all costs, as at once his wife would have begun to suspect something amiss. The latter he could do for a while without feeling it, but not for very long.

However, though Haslar was a good deal worried, he did not as yet consider his case really serious. So long as Blunt's demands remained anywhere about their present scale, he could meet them and carry on. Any small retrenchment that might be necessary he could account for by saying that his shares had fallen.

But now at last, within this very week, a fresh blow had fallen, by far the heaviest of all. It left Haslar stunned and desperate.

Blunt had once again rung up and asked to see him. Haslar supposed it meant some fresh extortion, but always afraid, that the old man might turn up at Oxshott, he had agreed to meet him at the rendezvous on the Great North Road. He had kept the appointment and had picked up Blunt in his car.

At once to his horror he saw that the man was drunk. He was not hopelessly incapacitated, but he was stupid and maudlin and spoke in a thick voice.

Here was a new and dreadful complication! To have his security at the mercy of an evil and selfish old man was bad enough: to have it in the keeping of a drunkard was a thousand times worse. In a certain stage of intoxication men of Blunt's type grew garrulous. Even if Blunt's intentions remained good, his actions were no longer dependable.

Haslar for the first time felt really up against it. His home, his wife, his friends, his pleasant circumstances, all were in danger. Never had his mode of life seemed so sweet as now that it was threatened. Security! That was what mattered. His security was gone. What would he not give to get it back!

And all this menacing misery and wretchedness would be the fate not only of himself but of his wife. Gina thought more of social prestige than he did. She would feel their disgrace the more. He had never told her he had been in jail. She would feel cheated. Not only would they be driven from their happy surroundings, but their own good comradeship would be gone. The more Haslar considered it, the more complete appeared the threatening ruin.

And all of it depended on the existence of one evil old man: a man guilty of the loathsome crime of blackmail: a man whose life was of no use or pleasure to himself or to anyone else: a man who was an encumbrance and a nuisance to all who knew him. It was not fair, Haslar thought bitterly. The happiness of two healthy and comparatively young people should not be in the power of this old sot.

And then the thought which for a long time had lurked in the recesses of Haslar's mind, forced itself to the front. It was not right that he and Gina should suffer. It was his job to see that Gina didn't suffer. Well, she needn't. She wouldn't – if Blunt were to die.

When first the dreadful idea leaped into his mind Haslar had crushed it out in horror. A murderer! No, not that! Anything rather than that! But the thought had returned. As often as he repulsed it, it came back. If Blunt were to die…

It would be a hideous, a ghastly affair, Blunt's dying. But if it were over? Haslar could scarcely conceive what the relief would be like. Security once again! An escape from his troubles!

But could he pay the price?

Haslar played with the horrible thought. But all the time, though he didn't realize it, his mind was made up. Blunt was old, he must die soon in any case. He was infirm, his life was no pleasure to him. A painless end. And for Haslar, security!

Then Haslar told himself that his solution mightn't mean security at all. There was another side to the picture. He broke into a cold sweat as he thought of the end of so many who had tried to attain security in this way. The sudden appearance of large men with official manners; the request to accompany them; the magistrates; the weeks of waiting; the trial. And then Haslar shuddered as he pictured what might follow. *That* was what had happened to so very many. Why should he escape?

Escape depended on the method employed. From that moment his thoughts became filled with the one idea – to find a plan. Was there any way in which he could bring about his release without fear of that awful result? Could murder be committed without paying the price?

He was convinced that it could – if only he could find the way.

III

Whatever Stewart Haslar undertook, he performed with system and efficiency. In considering any new enterprise, he began by defining in his mind the precise object he wished to obtain so as not to dissipate his energies on side issues. Then he made sure that he had an accurate knowledge of all the circumstances of the case and the factors which might affect his results. Only when he was thus prepared did he begin to consider plans of action. But when at last he reached this stage he gave every detail the closest attention, and he never passed from a scheme until he was satisfied it was as flawless as it was possible to make it. Finally, like a general planning a campaign, he considered in turn all the things which might go wrong, thinking out the correct action to be taken in each such emergency.

In this latest and most dreadful effort of his life, the murder of Henry Blunt, he pursued the same method. Here also he began by asking himself what did he want to attain?

This at least was an easy question. He wanted two things. First, he wanted Blunt to be dead. He wanted his tongue to be silenced in the only way that was entirely and absolutely effective. Secondly, he wanted this so to happen that no connection between himself and the murder would ever be suspected.

The next point was not so simple. What were the precise circumstances of the case and the factors which might affect his results?

First, as to his past dealings with Blunt. As things were, how far, if at all, could skilled detectives connect him with his victim?

He considered the point with care, and the more he did so the better pleased he became. He had been more discreet even than he had supposed. There was nothing that anyone could get hold of. He had always insisted on his communications with the old man being carried out secretly. When telephoning, Blunt never gave his name, ringing off after making his call unless he recognized Haslar's voice. Moreover, he always spoke from a street booth, so that his identity should remain untraceable. Haslar then had never allowed himself to be seen talking to the old man. Provided no one else was close by, he had stopped his car momentarily on an open stretch of the Great North Road, to pick Blunt up and set him down again. Sitting back in the closed car, he, Haslar, could not have been recognized even if there had been anyone to recognize him. During the drive it was unlikely that either of them would be recognized, but even supposing someone had seen them from a passing car, it was impossible that *both* should have been recognized, for the simple reason that no one knew both of them.

Haslar had been insistent that neither party should write to the other, and the only further way in which they came in contact was during the monthly payments. But these meetings Haslar was satisfied could not under any circumstances become known. In the first place, nothing could be learnt from the banknotes. They were all of the denomination of one pound and could not be traced. Moreover, Haslar never drew the whole £10 or £14 or £20 from his bank at one time, but collected the notes gradually. It was clearly understood that Blunt should not pay them into a bank, but should keep them at his cottage and use them for his current expenses. Finally, the method of utilizing the directory in the telephone booth at Victoria was secrecy itself. Not only was the booth in an inconspicuous place and neither man went to it if another user were present, but also they never spoke or communicated with one another in any visible way.

It seemed then to Haslar that so far as his dealings with Blunt in the past were concerned he was absolutely safe. But could Blunt have done anything which might call attention to him, Haslar?

Haslar didn't see how he could. Even if in a moment of carelessness Blunt had spoken of his rich friend, he would never have been so mad as to mention Haslar's name. Blunt knew perfectly well that the revelation of the secret would end its cash value to himself, that to give it away would be to kill the goose that was laying the golden eggs. Nor had Blunt a photograph or any paper which might lead to an identification.

Haslar again had been very careful not to appear in any of the negotiations the other had carried on. Blunt had bought the house and engaged the daily help. Except in an advisory capacity and in the secret passing of one pound banknotes via the Victoria telephone booth, Haslar had had no connection with any of Blunt's affairs.

So far everything seemed propitious, but there was one point which gave Haslar very furiously to think. Had Blunt written anywhere a statement of the truth, perhaps as a sort of guard against foul play?

This was a serious consideration. If such a document were in existence, to carry out his plan might be simply signing his own death warrant.

Haslar gave the point earnest thought and at last came to the conclusion that he need have no fears of such a contingency. Blunt would not be disposed to put his ugly secret in writing, lest the document should accidentally be found. For the truth would injure him in precisely the same way as it would Haslar. Besides losing Haslar's payments he also would personally suffer. If the circumstances under which he left Edinburgh became known, he also would be cold-shouldered out of his little circle of acquaintances. He wouldn't get a daily help or a welcome to the bar of the 'Green Goat'. Revelation would not be so disastrous as in Haslar's case, but still it would be pretty unpleasant.

Further and more convincingly, the only motive Blunt could have had for making a written statement would be that Haslar had already considered – as a safeguard against foul play. But this safeguard would be inoperative unless Haslar knew of its existence. Now Blunt had never mentioned such a document. This silence seemed to Haslar conclusive proof that nothing of the kind existed.

Reviewing the whole circumstances Haslar felt convinced that nothing had taken place in the past which could possibly connect him with Blunt. So far, so good. But what of the future? Could a method of murder be devised which would leave him equally dissociated?

This wasn't an easy problem. The more Haslar thought over it, the more impossible it seemed. To murder Blunt involved becoming associated with him. The man would have to be met, personally. Haslar began to visualize picking him up on the Great North Road on the occasion of his next demand, and driving him to some lonely spot where the dreadful deed could be carried out and the body hidden. But this would be horribly dangerous. He, Haslar, might be seen; he might drop something traceable; the car might be observed; the wheel marks might be found. The whole thing indeed was bristling with risks. And if he, Haslar, were asked where he was at the time, what should he say? He could put up no alibi and the absence of one would be fatal.

But was he not going too fast? Had he considered all the circumstances of Blunt's life? To do so might give him the hint he required.

He had never seen the cottage bought with his money, but Blunt had shown him a photograph and described it. It was a small bungalow with three rooms, which Blunt used as kitchen, sitting-room and bedroom. It had electric light and water, but not gas. It stood in a field alongside a lane, surrounded by trees and with a tiny garden. It was very secluded and yet was within a hundred yards of a main road. Anything might happen there unknown to neighbours or passers-by. A shot could even be fired with a fair chance of its being unheard.

Haslar considered paying the place a nocturnal visit. He could park up the lane, knock at the door, hit Blunt over the head when he opened it, and drive back to Oxshott. He might manage that part of it all right. But he could never get secretly away from home. Gina would wake and miss him. The taking out of the car might be heard. No, that didn't seem a possibility.

His thoughts returned to Blunt. How did the old man spend his day? Here again his information was scanty. The picture he was able to build up from the few remarks Blunt had dropped was incomplete. And yet he knew so much that he thought he could fill in the blanks.

The first thing which took place in the morning was the arrival of Mrs Parrott, the daily help. She prepared breakfast and when Blunt came down it was waiting for him. During the morning she cleaned the house, prepared Blunt's midday and evening meals and left them ready for him to heat, and washed up the previous day's dishes. She left about noon. Blunt smoked, read the paper, listened to his wireless, went down to the 'Green Goat', pottered in the garden, or went for a bus ride as the humour took him. He warmed up his evening meal and retired to bed, where he read himself to sleep.

He was not, so Blunt had himself said, socially inclined. The 'Green Goat' gave him all the companionship he wanted. Seldom or never did he offer hospitality to his neighbours.

It was beginning to look to Haslar as if the only way he could carry out his dreadful purpose was by an evening or night visit. By parking some distance away and walking to the cottage he might manage the actual murder safely enough. But he couldn't see how to overcome the difficulty of getting away from Oxshott. The more he thought of this, the more insuperable it seemed.

For days Haslar pondered his problem. Under all the special circumstances of Blunt's life, was there no way in which the man could be removed with secrecy? He could think of none.

And then one morning an idea suddenly flashed into his mind. Was there not, after all, a very obvious way in which a man could be done to death with complete and absolute safety to the murderer?

Haslar's heart began to beat more rapidly. He sat stiffly forward, thinking intently. Yes, he believed there was such a way. Admittedly it would only work under certain circumstances, but in this case these circumstances obtained.

He went to his table and picked up a book a friend had lent him. It was a popular account of the application of science to detection and told of the use that is being made of such things as fingerprints, the microscopic examination of dust, ultra-violet photography, chemical analysis and criminal psychology. Eagerly he turned the pages. He thought he remembered the details of what he had read, but he must check himself. He found the paragraph.

Yes, he was right. The method he had in mind was very commonly used by criminals. It had been tested a good many times and was foolproof. Of course he would not use it exactly as it had been used before. He would add his own modification, and it was this modification which would make the affair so absolutely safe.

Safe! By this plan he would be as secure as if he took no action at all. He could never be suspected. But even if he were suspected, even if Blunt left a statement of the secret, he was safe. If the police were convinced of his guilt he was safe. Never, under any circumstances, could they prove what he had done.

If Blunt's fate had been in doubt before, it was now sealed beyond yea or nay.

IV

To Stewart Haslar his idea as to how Henry Blunt might be safely murdered soon became an impersonal problem like those he had dealt with when managing his chain stores in Australia. Once its thrill and horror had worn off he set to work on it with his customary systematic thoroughness. He began by a general consideration of the details of the plan and then made out a list of the various things he had to do. In the main these consisted of three items: he had to buy or otherwise obtain certain materials; he had to make a certain piece of apparatus; and he had to ensure that Blunt would do nothing to upset the scheme.

The most risky part of the plan was the purchase of two chemicals. One was easy to obtain, the other might be more difficult. He decided to begin by buying these, as if he failed on this point he need proceed no further.

Carefully he worked out two disguises. He invariably appeared in tweed suits and Homburg hats. In a large establishment in the City he bought a ready-made suit of black and a cheap bowler, and in a second-hand clothes shop an old fawn waterproof and a cap. He did not wear glasses: therefore in a theatrical supplies shop he secured a couple of spectacles, both with plain glass, but one with dark rims and the other with light. From a piece of soft rubber insertion he cut two tiny pairs of differently shaped pads for his cheeks. All these, together with a brush and comb, he packed in a suitcase, which he placed in his car.

On the next convenient day he drove to Town, saying he would lunch at his club and do some shopping. He did both of these: lunched with acquaintances, who in case of need would certify that he was there, and bought a number of articles which he could, and afterwards did, show to his wife. But he did more.

In the car he put on the old waterproof, which he buttoned up round his neck. He took off his hat, brushed his hair back from front to rear in a way in which he never wore it, put on the cap and light spectacles, and slipped one pair of the rubber pads into his cheeks. Thus prepared, he set out.

On a previous occasion he had noted two or three large chemists' shops near Paddington and Liverpool Street respectively. Selecting one near Paddington, he parked in an adjoining street and walked round. As he had hoped, it was well filled with customers.

'I want a little potassium chlorate, please,' he said, 'to mix my own gargle.'

'Potassium chlorate, yes,' the assistant returned. 'About what quantity?'

Haslar made a gesture indicating a package about 3 ins x 2 ins x 2 ins. 'I don't know,' he admitted. 'I suppose about that size.'

The assistant nodded and weighed out the white powder, handed over the little package, gave the change, said 'Good afternoon' in the usually politely perfunctory manner, and turned to serve the next customer. Haslar walked quietly out. The first of his two principal fences was taken!

But this first was easy. The second, which he was now going to attempt, was the most difficult and dangerous item in his whole programme.

Having walked to Paddington, he went with his suitcase into the station lavatory and there changed to his black suit and bowler hat. He rebrushed his hair, put on the dark-rimmed spectacles and exchanged the pads in his cheeks. Then, slipping out while the attendant's back was turned, he regained the car and drove to Liverpool Street. Again he parked at a convenient distance and walked to another of the chemists.

'I want some picric acid for burns, please. The powder, if you have it. I like to make up my own ointment.'

The assistant looked along his shelves. 'We have it, in solution,' he said, 'and on gauze. I'm afraid we're out of the powder.'

This was what Haslar had feared. 'Then give me the gauze,' he answered. 'It'll do well enough.'

He bought a roll of gauze which he didn't want, stored it in the car, parked in a new place and tried a second shop. He was prepared to go on visiting shop after shop for the entire afternoon, but to his delight, at this second establishment he got what he wanted. Without any formality or suggestion that his request was unusual, he obtained a small bottle of the brilliant yellow powder. As this seemed scarcely enough, he got a second bottle in another shop.

Six more purchases Haslar made before changing back to his normal garb. One was at still another chemist's. There he bought a dozen small test tubes, about 3 ins long by ¼ in. diameter, and a dozen rubber 'corks' to fit. The second was at a garage, where he got a small bottle of sulphuric acid, 'to top up my batteries'. The third purchase was a couple of sheets of brown paper and the fourth a ball of twine, both at small stationers. The fifth and sixth were a steel pen and a cheap bottle of ink, each obtained at a different establishment.

Haslar breathed more freely as he reached home and locked his purchases in his safe. His great difficulty had been overcome. He had obtained everything that he required to complete his apparatus. A mixture of potassium chlorate and picric acid was inert and harmless, but this mixture in contact with sulphuric acid became a powerful explosive. He believed he had enough chemicals to blow half his house to pieces. And he had obtained them *secretly*. He was satisfied that his purchases had attracted no special attention and that under no circumstances could they be traced to him.

The next step was to make his apparatus. He was something of a carpenter and metal worker and he had a fair outfit of tools in his workshop.

Wearing his rubber gloves, he took some ⅜ in. plywood and made himself a small flat box with outside dimensions of about the size of an ordinary novel. One of the long edges he made to open on a hinge and to fasten with a small hook and eye. He was careful not to use a plane or chisel, as he was aware that cuts made by these tools could be identified.

Before fastening on the sides he made and fixed the operating machinery. This consisted of a steel lever some 3 inches long, with one end bent round and chisel-pointed and mounted on a pivot at the opposite end so that the pointed end could swing from close to the lid to near the base. A strong spring coiled round the pivot kept the lever down in the latter position. Fastened to the base beneath the unpivoted end of the lever was a little block of oak to act as an anvil. The arrangement was that if the lever were lifted towards the lid and let go, it would immediately snap its chisel-point down on the anvil.

Through the sides Haslar bored a hole so that if the lever were raised towards the lid, a pin pushed through these holes would keep it in that position. To the lid he fixed a small projecting lug of steel, so that when the lid was closed it would come down in front of the raised lever and prevent it dropping. Haslar's original diagrammatic sketch of the apparatus is reproduced below.

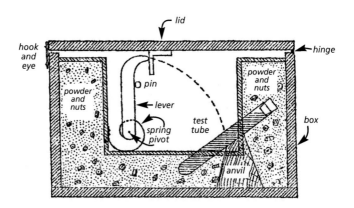

Haslar now conducted some tests. First he raised the lever, slipping in the pin to hold it in place. Filling a test tube with water, he corked it and fastened it in the box across the anvil. Then he closed the lid and withdrew the pin. Driven by the spring, the lever slipped forward till it was held by the lug projecting from the lid.

Then Haslar raised the lid. This freed the lever from the lug, it snapped down on the anvil, smashed the test tube into fragments, and spilled the water.

Haslar was delighted. He repeated the experiment several times. Not once did the raising of the lid fail to break the test tube.

Then he put in his chemicals. Having pinned up the lever, he put some sulphuric acid into a test tube and secured it firmly on the anvil. Next he mixed the white potassium chlorate with the yellow picric acid and filled it in, inserting also a number of old bolt nuts to act as projectiles.

Thin wooden divisions kept the powder from getting out of place and preventing the lever from falling.

With the utmost care Haslar now closed the lid, hooked it fast and withdrew the pin. Then, taking a sheet of his brown paper, he parcelled up the box, finally tying it with a length of his twine.

One further operation remained, one to which he had given a lot of thought. He must address his parcel. But if it should happen that the parcel fell into the hands of the police, the writing must not be traceable to himself.

A box of sporting cartridges had reached him a few days earlier, of which the label had been addressed in block capitals. He had kept this label, and now, using his steel pen and the cheap ink, he set himself to copy the letters. Slowly he printed:

MR SAMUEL JAMISON,
"GORSEFIELD,"
HENNIKER ROAD,
RICKMANSWORTH,
NR LONDON.

Then he weighed the parcel and put on the required stamps.

Locking away the box in his safe, he proceeded to destroy all traces of what he had done. The remainder of the plywood, the sporting cartridge label, the brown paper, the ball of string and his rubber gloves he burnt, scattering the ashes. The test tubes, the bottles which had held the chemicals, the pen and ink and all the remaining nuts he threw into the nearest river. He was careful to see that nothing he had used in connection with the affair remained.

Nothing left to connect him with the affair! And if the bomb failed to go off, nothing about it traceable and no fingerprints anywhere upon it! So far he was absolutely safe!

The third part of his scheme only remained: to make sure that Blunt would open the box. This he had already arranged. At their last interview he had brought the conversation round to the question of the furnishing of Blunt's cottage and had learnt that the man was badly off for a clock. Any other small object would have done equally well, and Haslar would have gone on talking till one was mentioned. But a clock was entirely suitable.

'Oh,' he said, 'I have a clock that I don't want. It's a small thin one, little bigger than a watch in a stand, but beautifully made. I'll bring it along next time I see you. Or rather I'll send it, for I'm going to be away from home for a few weeks.'

As he had anticipated, Blunt's greed blinded him to Haslar's departure from his usual refusal to use the post. Haslar described the sort of parcel he would send and he had no doubt Blunt would immediately open it.

And when he opened it! An explosion! Swift and painless death! Complete destruction of the parcel: perhaps complete destruction of the cottage, a fire might easily be started. And under no circumstances could anything be connected with him, Haslar!

Going again to lunch in Town, Haslar slipped the parcel into the large letter-box of a post office on his way to the club. It would be delivered that evening – when Blunt would be alone in the house.

That evening Haslar would be free.

V

Stewart Haslar had supposed that once he had posted his bomb, his personal interest in the death of Henry Blunt would be over. He soon found he had been mistaken. It was from that moment, when action was over, that his real anxiety began.

While he was lunching at his club things were not so bad. Several hours must elapse before anything could happen, and the conversation of his friends helped him to put the affair to some extent out of his mind. But as the afternoon dragged on and the time for the evening delivery at Rickmansworth drew near, he found he could no longer control his agitation.

On the way home he realized that his excited state of mind could not fail to attract his wife's attention. This, he saw even more clearly still, would be a disaster. Under no circumstances must she be allowed to suspect that he had anything special on his mind.

For a time he simply tried to force himself to forget what he had done. To some extent he succeeded, but in spite of all his efforts, he found he could not make his manner normal.

His longing to know what had happened grew till it became positive pain. Over and over again he pictured the probable scene. The postman's knock, Blunt opening the door, a word or two about the weather, Blunt returning to his sitting-room, unwrapping the paper, opening the lid… And then what? Was Blunt dead? Was the box and paper burnt? Was the cottage burnt? Had anyone yet discovered the affair? Haslar, his hands shaking, grew more and more upset. For the first time in his life he understood the urge which tends to drive a murderer back to the scene of his crime.

He wondered how he could find out what really was taking place, then sweated in horror that such a thought should have come to him. He couldn't find out. Above all things, he mustn't try. He could read the papers he was accustomed to read, and those only. If there was nothing about the affair in them he would have to remain in ignorance.

But curse it all, he told himself, he *must* know. He must know if he was safe. Up till now he had never for a moment doubted that the explosion would kill Blunt instantaneously. But now fears assailed him. He began to picture the man in hospital – recovering. *And knowing who sent the parcel.*

Haslar stopped the car. He was sweating and trembling. This would never do. He had carried out a perfect plan and he must not wreck it now by lack of self-control. Then he saw that it was all very well to think such thoughts. The thing was stronger than he was. His anxiety was insupportable and he could not hide it.

As he sat thinking, he suddenly saw his way. He was still within the limits of Town and he stopped at the first grocer's he came to and bought a package of common salt. With this he thought he could prevent any suspicion arising.

Arrived at his home, he garaged the car and went to his room. There with the salt he prepared himself an emetic. Putting it beside him, he lay down on his bed.

Gina, he knew, had been going out in the afternoon and the absence of her car told him that she had not yet returned. He lay waiting. Then at last he heard the car. At once he drank the salt and water, washed the glass and left it in its place, and lay down again. When shortly afterwards Gina came upstairs, he was just being violently sick.

She was upset about it, for such an attack was unusual.

'It's all right,' he assured her. 'Must have had something that disagreed with me for lunch. Been feeling seedy all afternoon. I'll be better now.'

She wanted to send for the doctor, but this he scouted. Then she insisted on his lying on his bed and not going down for dinner. He protested, but with secret satisfaction gave way. The lowering effect of the sickness had reduced his nervousness so that he really felt practically normal. He was sure his manner was unsuspicious.

Next morning he found it a matter of extreme difficulty to avoid rushing down the drive and snatching the paper from the newsboy. But he managed to restrain himself. He did not open it till his normal time, and then he forced himself to make his usual comments on the outstanding news before slowly turning away from the centre pages.

He was on tenterhooks as he searched the sheets. If anything had gone wrong with his scheme and Blunt had escaped, there would be no paragraph. If the plan had succeeded perfectly so that only accident was suspected, there might be no paragraph. Only would a notice be certain if a partial success had taken place: if Blunt had died, but under suspicion of foul play.

Then on an early page Haslar saw a short paragraph. It was headed 'FATAL EXPLOSION', and read: 'Through an explosion in his cottage last evening, Mr Samuel Jamison, Henniker Road, Rickmansworth, lost his life. The report was heard by a passer-by who entered and found Jamison lying in his wrecked sitting-room. The cause of the explosion is unknown.'

Haslar had now almost as much trouble in hiding his relief as before he had had in covering his anxiety. Cause unknown! This was better than anything he could have hoped for. He had a convenient fit of coughing and by the time it was over he felt himself once again under control.

All that day he oscillated between exultation and fear. To steady his nerves he went for a long tramp. But he was careful to be back when the evening paper arrived. The only fresh news was that the inquest was to be held that afternoon.

Another night of suspense and another period of stress in the morning and Haslar was once again turning the sheets of the paper. This time he had less difficulty in finding what he was looking for. Almost at once his eye caught ominous headlines. With a sinking feeling he devoured the report, which was unusually detailed. It read:

THE RICKMANSWORTH FATALITY
STARTLING DEVELOPMENT

At the inquest yesterday afternoon at Rickmansworth on the body of Samuel Jamison, Gorsefield, Henniker Road, who died as the result of an explosion in his cottage on the previous evening, the possibility of foul play was suggested.

James Richardson said that at about six o'clock when walking close to the deceased's bungalow, he heard an explosion and saw a window blown out. He climbed in and found the deceased lying dead on the floor. The room was wrecked and bore traces of yellow powder. Witness telephoned for the police.

Mrs Martha Parrott, who worked for the deceased, deposed that he was between sixty and seventy and had lived in the neighbourhood for some three years. He was solitary in his habits and appeared to have no relatives. She was positive there was nothing in the house to account for the explosion.

Thomas Kent, postman, said that on his evening delivery just before the explosion he had handed deceased a small brown-paper parcel. It was addressed in block letters and had a London postmark. He had remarked upon it particularly, as Mr Jamison's correspondence was so small.

Sergeant Allsopp stated that the police were of opinion that the explosive was contained in the parcel, which would suggest the possibility of foul play. The proceedings were adjourned for the police to make inquiries.

★   ★   ★

With a supreme effort Haslar recalled himself to his surroundings. Gina was speaking of the following weekend and he forced himself to discuss with her the arrangements they would make for the entertainment of their guests. But after breakfast he retired to the solitude of his study and gave himself over to considering the situation.

It really was more satisfactory than it had seemed at first sight. After all, though this idea of the police was unfortunate, he had expected it. An explosion of the kind could not possibly be considered an accident unless there were known explosives in the house. There were none at Blunt's. Moreover, that cursed picric acid had made yellow stains. For all Haslar knew to the contrary those stains could be analysed and shown to be picric. This would prove the explosive had been sent to the house, and the parcel was the obvious way. No, it was inherent in the scheme that the police should suspect foul play.

But that would do him, Haslar, no harm. It was one thing to suspect the parcel was a bomb: it was quite another to find the sender. There was nothing by which the police could discover that 'Jamison' was Blunt who had disappeared from Edinburgh – he had never been through their hands. Therefore even if they knew that he, Haslar, was Matthews – which was extremely unlikely – it would get them no further. Besides, even if a miracle happened and the police did suspect him, they couldn't prove anything. They couldn't connect him with the purchase of the chemicals or the construction of the bomb or show that he posted the parcel.

No, it was a dreadfully anxious time, of course, but he was safe. Haslar repeated the words over and over again to himself. He was safe! He was safe! No matter what the police tried to do, he was safe.

THE MOTIVE SHOWS THE MAN

In many unsolved murder mysteries, the true difficulty which has confronted the police is not that of finding the criminal, or the person who is most probably the criminal, but that of proving his guilt in a way which will convince a jury.

Mr Freeman Wills Crofts, however, presents the Hertfordshire police with a problem in which, at the point where his narrative ends, there appears to be nothing to point to the identity of the murderer.

I congratulate Mr Crofts on his ingenuity in devising what must, at first reading, appear to the ordinary man or woman to be a 'perfect murder'. But, in real life, although the detectives in charge of the case would certainly find it difficult, I am by no means convinced that they would be forced to abandon it as insoluble.

They begin their investigation with the knowledge of certain facts which suggests a definite line of inquiry.

The crime was committed by a person with some knowledge of chemistry.

That person had some very strong motive, which was not robbery, and must be explained by the relations between the murderer and his victim. Therefore, the criminal was known to, or connected with, the dead man in some way.

The parcel had been posted in London. Possibly, though that was not stated in the report of the inquest, the postal district had been noted by the postman. Or the postmark might be reconstructed from the fragments of the box which remained.

These facts seem little enough, but they would be supplemented very quickly.

Suppose that I were the detective in charge of the case. I should first examine the body and note any scars or other distinguishing marks. Then I should go through the clothing very carefully. Probably I should first find nothing that was helpful. But either in his pockets, or somewhere in the cottage, which would be thoroughly searched, I should discover the balance of his last monthly payment.

This was at least £20 pounds and it had been made only a few days previously. The reason Haslar gave for sending the parcel by post had been that he was to be away for a few weeks. The conditions of the monthly rendezvous meant that this could only happen just after a payment. Otherwise, the blackmailer would immediately have demanded his next month's money.

I should therefore find quite a substantial sum in £1 notes – perhaps £15, almost certainly not less than £10. And I should learn, on making inquiries, that Jamison had no banking account, that he did no work, and that he paid for everything he bought in cash, but never with notes of a higher denomination than £1. Further, I would ascertain that he had had more money towards the end of his residence at Rickmansworth than at the beginning of it, and that he had recently purchased an expensive radiogram and an assortment of records, again paying in £1 notes.

Trying to discover the source of his income, I should find myself up against a blank wall. But the mystery surrounding this would itself tell me something. There had been something shady about Jamison and his money.

One of my main sources of information would naturally be Mrs Parrott. She would tell me all that she knew, and a good deal that she had guessed. Her guesses would probably be wrong, but if Jamison had had any visitors, or if there was any relative or friend with whom he was in touch, she might be able to assist me considerably. True, I would not get a line on Haslar in this way, because of the precautions he had taken; but I might uncover the secret of Jamison's identity, which would lead me, in the end, to Haslar.

In any case, I should discover that Jamison had gone up to town on the first Monday of each month. I might even learn that, on at least some of these occasions, he had gone to Victoria. And I should be inclined to associate these journeys to London with his source of income.

The possibility of blackmail would be present in my mind. But I would not rule out other forms of crime. In any case it would be useful to know if Jamison had a criminal record. I would have his fingerprints taken and sent to Scotland Yard.

Haslar had thought there was nothing by which Jamison could be identified by the police as Blunt the Edinburgh bank clerk – he had never been through their hands. But Blunt had been down and out when he crossed Haslar's path for the second time, and he had already been a crook, though he had avoided arrest, when he was in Edinburgh. During the thirty-five years' interval between these two events, had he gone straight? It was hardly likely. And almost certainly, if he had been on the wrong side of the law, he had been found out and had been punished.

In the cottage I should have looked carefully for any letters, diaries, notebooks – any scrap of writing that might help to throw light on Jamison's past. But even if I found nothing, even if Mrs Parrott could tell me nothing, it is a hundred to one that, Jamison's character being what it was, his fingerprints would be in the records. And though he told Haslar that he had changed his name on leaving Edinburgh, he might have been convicted as Blunt, or his identity with Blunt might have been established.

If this were so, it would be only a matter of time before inquiries by the Edinburgh police would bring to light the story of Matthews and suggest a possible motive for the murder.

I should still have to trace Matthews and might find that a very difficult and laborious business. But was there no one – no relative or friend – who knew that Matthews had changed his name to Haslar and gone out to Australia? Had no one, before that meeting with Blunt, ever recognized him as Matthews?

It is at least possible that, even with no fortunate chance to help me, I should be able, in the end, to lay bare the whole story of Matthews' struggle and success as Haslar in Australia, and of his return to England.

But there might easily be a short cut to this – the fortunate chance to which I referred above.

I have so far assumed that, in my search of the cottage, I found no scrap of writing that could throw light on my problem. I have also ignored the possibility of Jamison having been in communication with some relative or friend. Let us say now, definitely, that there was no relative with whom he had been in touch – no one, except Haslar, who knew that Jamison and Blunt were one and the same. There was still one person with whom Jamison had communicated – Haslar himself. In a pocket diary, or on a scrap of paper, I might find Haslar's address, or – what would be just as good and perhaps more likely – his telephone number.

It was always by telephone that Jamison made appointments with Haslar. He would probably remember the number after asking for it once or twice, but he would naturally note it somewhere the first time he used it. And while Haslar had a powerful motive for destroying everything that might link him in any way with Jamison, the latter had no such motive where Haslar was concerned.

When planning the murder, Haslar wondered if, perhaps, the blackmailer had committed his secret to writing. He dismissed the idea because the document might be found by a third party, in which case Jamison would himself have been in an unpleasant position. But a telephone number would give nothing away while Jamison still lived – though it might take on significance after his murder.

That was a vital point Haslar had overlooked.

He had also failed to reckon with another possibility. After he had handed Jamison the money to buy his radiogram, we are told that the old man's demands increased till Haslar was parting with quite a considerable proportion of his income. It is not clear whether the monthly payments were larger or whether there were other and more frequent demands for lump sums, but, beyond the fact that he was drinking more heavily, there is no indication of any change in Jamison's mode of life, nor are we told of any other large purchase which he made.

Having regard to all the circumstances, it is possible that Jamison was accumulating a reserve. After all, Haslar, though his junior, was no longer young. He might die. He might be killed in an accident. And with his death Jamison would once more be thrown on his own resources.

The blackmailer would not keep his reserve in his cottage. He would know that this was too dangerous. He had no local bank account, Haslar was probably correct in thinking that he had no bank account at all. Banks usually want references from a new customer. But there was no reason why he should not rent a strongbox in a safe deposit. There he could place, not only his reserve, but also any papers he wanted to keep in readiness for possible emergencies.

He need not have written any account of his dealings with Haslar. But suppose he had obtained, from the offices of an Edinburgh newspaper, a photographic copy of the report of Matthews' trial and had placed that in the safe deposit. It might be useful to show to Haslar one day, if he was inclined to kick against the pricks.

Say, then, that in my search of the cottage, I found, in the pocket of an old suit, a scrap of paper with a telephone number. No name might be attached to it, but I would soon ascertain whose number it was and, as a matter of routine, Haslar would be interviewed, and asked if he had known Jamison.

Haslar had been living under an almost intolerable strain ever since his meeting with the blackmailer. His conduct at the time of the murder and immediately afterwards was that of a man who was near to breaking-point. Now, when he has got over his panic, when he thinks he is safe, he is suddenly confronted with a police officer, and realizes that, in some way, a connection between himself and Jamison has been established.

He does not know exactly what the detectives have discovered. He probably thinks their researches are much further advanced than, in fact, they are. His reaction will almost inevitably arouse suspicion. He will betray agitation. Perhaps he will bluster.

But he will deny all knowledge of Jamison, and his family and servants, when questioned, will do the same.

Suppose that I have decided that this clue may be important and have gone to Oxshott myself. I have noted Haslar's agitation. Naturally, I accept what he says. But I tell him that I am anxious to learn who Jamison actually was – that I have reason to suspect that this wasn't his real name. Would Mr Haslar come with me and see if he could identify the body?

This might conceivably result in the murderer going to pieces altogether, and the whole truth coming out. In any case, by the time that our interview had finished, Haslar would again be in a state of panic, and I would know that he had something to conceal.

Now if, in addition to the telephone number, I had found a safe deposit key, and the strong box contained particulars of Matthews' trial in addition to securities, I would be able to guess what the connection between Haslar and Jamison was, and have a very good idea of the motive of the murder.

I should therefore have some very interesting questions to put to Haslar at our next interview. The answers would probably be lies, but that wouldn't matter. He would be definitely under suspicion, and police officers would be detailed to watch his movements. If he attempted to leave the country, he would be detained – and I would know definitely that he was the man I wanted.

Meantime, every fragment that I had been able to pick up of the box which had contained the explosive and the wrappings in which it had arrived, would have been examined by experts. However small these fragments, they might have a story to tell, and nothing of this would escape the trained scientists who did this part of the work.

There might be some link here that could be established, in spite of all his precautions, between Haslar and the crime. I know that 'he was careful to see that nothing he had used in connection with the affair remained.' Robinson, of the Charing Cross trunk crime, was careful to see that no trace was left in his office of the murder of Mrs Bonati, but after all his labour a bloodstained match and a hairpin were found in his wastepaper basket and helped to hang him.

Haslar's workshop would certainly be searched. It might yield nothing. But even then it would still be possible that someone, himself unseen, had watched the murderer at his work of destroying the evidence and would come forward as soon as he realized that the incident which had puzzled him had a bearing on the crime.

Am I making things too easy for the detective by imagining all these possibilities? Even if none of my 'fortunate chances' materialized, once it had been established that Jamison was really Blunt, ordinary police routine work would establish the connection with Matthews and trace the latter. It would take longer, but it would be done in the end.

But if Jamison had led a life of crime, there might be others besides Matthews who had a possible motive for desiring his death. They would all be traced and eliminated one by one. And with every suspect who satisfied the detectives that he could have had nothing to do with the crime, the unmasking of the real murderer would be brought a step nearer.

I have mentioned certain contingencies, however, in order to show that Haslar, when he thought he was planning the perfect murder, was very far indeed from doing so. There were too many unknown factors in Jamison's life for the crime to be safe.

And even now I have left out of account what was, perhaps, the most immediate danger of all – and one which Haslar must have realized, if he had thought intelligently about his problem at all.

He decided to kill Jamison, not because he was blackmailing him, but because he was a drunkard. 'In a certain stage of intoxication men of Blunt's type grew garrulous. Even if Blunt's intentions remained good, his actions were no longer dependable.'

So the blackmailer was killed to prevent him blurting out his secret while under the influence of alcohol. But how could Haslar be sure that he hadn't done so already? How many times had he been drunk before Haslar saw him in that condition? How many times was he drunk between that incident and the murder?

Possibly he had thrown out hints, even mentioned names. No one might have paid any attention to what he said at the time, dismissing it as the maudlin raving of the inebriate. But the moment he was murdered it would assume a new and sinister significance. It would be recalled and repeated.

Those disguises, too, which Haslar put on to make his purchases, might actually have fixed the transactions in the minds of the chemists at whose shops he called. Nothing is so conspicuous as a disguise, when assumed by a person who is not accustomed to masquerade. And his altered appearance extended to a few details only – height, build and age were not affected.

The evidence of the shopkeepers, therefore, while it would not, of itself, lead to Haslar, would do nothing to destroy the case against him. On the contrary, it would add another link to the chain.

But suppose that, in the end, when every clue had been followed up, that chain was still one link short. I might know Haslar's history, I might be able to prove the blackmail and consequently the motive, but still be unable to show, to the satisfaction of a jury, that it was actually this man, and no other, who had prepared and posted the fatal parcel.

Even then I might still get him. I would go to him with the statements which he had made to me in the course of the investigation. I might be able to point to discrepancies between those he had made at different dates. I would undoubtedly be able to show that, in certain particulars, the story he had told me was at variance with facts which I had ascertained elsewhere. I would ask him for an explanation.

I think I would get the truth. I think that the long nervous strain which he had undergone would culminate, that this would snap and that he would confess. The customary warning would make no difference – he would not realize that he was fastening the rope round his own neck. He would think it was there already.

But suppose he didn't confess. I might still arrest him, knowing that the news of the arrest might bring in fresh information.

One of my first facts was that the murderer had some knowledge of chemistry. So far I have been unable to discover that Haslar had such knowledge. But after his arrest his friend comes forward, as a matter of public duty, and says: 'A week or two before the murder I lent Haslar this book. As you will see, it contains a description of the method which was followed in making the bomb that killed Jamison.'

Another link in the chain.

Then, it may be, someone appears who has seen Haslar post the parcel. He remembers the incident and the date because it struck him afterwards, reading the newspaper reports, that it must have been just such a parcel which had caused Jamison's death. But he did not think it was *the* parcel until he saw Haslar's photograph in the newspaper.

And so the case is completed, goes before judge and jury. I think there is little doubt what the verdict will be.

THE AFFAIR AT SALTOVER PRIORY

Upon three occasions only during the whole course of his career did the cases of Inspector French come to him otherwise than through the appointed channels of the Yard. Of these three exceptions that of the affair at Saltover Priory was from many points of view the most interesting.

It occurred during the great period of French's year – his summer holidays. At Saltover, in Devon, he had found a fair approximation to earthly bliss. There was delightful loafing in the sun, there was bathing, there were walks and 'sharry' excursions, there was a cinema and a good library of fiction. Moreover, the local sergeant, with whom French had soon made friends, owned a boat, and had delightedly initiated him into the mysteries and joys of sea fishing.

For three whole weeks French had intended to rid his thoughts of crime and of criminals, of inquiries and reports, of numbered exhibits and evidence, and to give himself up to the glorious freedom of his holiday. Up till that morning he had succeeded. But that morning tragedy had once again come within his purview. His landlady, her eyes starting from her head, had greeted him with the account of a suicide which had taken place on the previous evening. It was that of a local magnate, Sir Charles Goodliffe, who lived at the Priory, a fine house standing in its own grounds a little farther along the shore. French had seen him passing, a tall hatchet-faced man, thin and stooped as if from chronic illness. He had also seen Lady

Goodliffe, an athletic woman with a swinging gait and good features. Sir Charles, it appeared, had shot himself in his study. The servants and Lady Goodliffe, hearing the report, had rushed in and found him dead.

French frankly was not interested. He shocked the good landlady by his detachment, though when he explained that he had to deal with that sort of thing for forty-nine weeks in the year and was now on holiday, she admitted doubtfully that she could understand his attitude.

But French was not to escape. After lunch Sergeant Headley called in to say that he was sorry that owing to the tragedy he could not go out fishing that evening. 'You've heard about it, I suppose?' he went on, and though French reassured him, he insisted on recapitulating the details. To the sergeant the affair was evidently a major event. Sir Charles had been a rich man, a great churchman, and an outstanding figure in the district, and his death had aroused correspondingly widespread interest.

'Got the motive?' asked French, feeling he must play up to the story.

'Well no, Mr French,' Headley answered. Then he dropped his voice and became confidential. 'There are whispers about the wife and a man called Pettigrew, a rich landed proprietor who lives a mile or so away, but whether the deceased took them to heart or had even heard them, I don't know.'

'As a protest,' French returned, 'suicide strikes me as a bit drastic. Not many husbands take their lives nowadays for the loss of their wives' love.'

'He was old-fashioned, and it would have seemed to him like a family disgrace,' the sergeant explained. For some moments he enlarged on this theme, then with another apology about the fishing, said he must be getting on.

As his broad back disappeared French congratulated himself that he had now heard the last of the affair. In a place the size of Saltover he could understand that the suicide of one of the leading inhabitants would be a nine days' wonder. But for him it was anathema. He had only his three weeks, and in them he wanted to bathe not only his body but his mind in the fresh cleanness of sea and air and sun.

For the second time he was disappointed. On the following morning the tragedy was again brought to his notice, and by a very unexpected person.

He was sitting in the sunshine in front of his landlady's cottage when a car drove up and the driver, introducing himself as Lady Goodliffe's chauffeur, asked if he was addressing Inspector French. 'Her ladyship's compliments,' he went on, 'and she'd be grateful if you could speak to her. She's in the car.'

French walked across. Lady Goodliffe, he now saw, was a very pretty woman. Normally he fancied she would be reserved and distant, but at present she was too much agitated to be otherwise than natural. She leant forward and spoke impulsively.

'I heard you were here on holiday, Inspector. I felt I must speak to you.'

French raised his hat. 'Yes, madam. What can I do for you?'

'I know that when you're on holiday it's not fair to trouble you with business,' she returned, her hands working nervously, 'but I can't help it. I must take my chance when I see it.'

For the first time French felt a dawning interest in the tragedy. She was a very attractive looking woman and her voice was charming. He would certainly help her if he could. He bowed.

'I'm in dreadful trouble,' she continued falteringly. 'This terrible affair – you've heard of it? My husband?...'

'I've heard of it, madam, but not in any detail.'

'You've heard what they're saying?'

French shook his head.

'Such – dreadful things – about me.' She hesitated then went on as if taking a disagreeable plunge. 'They're saying – it was my fault, that – it happened. They're saying that I – that Mr Pettigrew and I – were too much together – that it upset my husband till he took his life. But I swear there's not one word of truth in it!'

French murmured politely. 'But what, madam, do you wish me to do in the matter?' he added.

'I want you,' she said earnestly, 'if you will, to find out the real reason – why he did it. I assure you it was not – what is being said.' She had spoken with an obvious reluctance, but now her words came more freely. 'Mr Pettigrew and I are friends, but nothing more. My husband knew we were friends and didn't disapprove. My husband and I were always fond of each other. He must have had some other motive. Will you look into it for me? I can pay any reasonable fee.'

French shook his head. 'I'm sorry, madam, but I'm afraid things are not arranged like that. I am not my own master, but the servant of the Yard. The local police have the matter in hand, and they will do all that is required. Speak to Sergeant Headley and he'll help you.'

She made a little gesture of despair. 'I have, but I could see he didn't believe me. It was such a chance your being here. I had hoped you could see your way...'

French was polite, but firm, and presently, with evident disappointment, she drove off. He was sorry for her and would have helped her had he had any choice in the matter.

But of course he had none. He couldn't butt into a case without instructions. All the same, he wondered what Headley had thought of her request.

He was soon to learn. Twenty minutes later the sergeant himself hove in sight, riding home for lunch from the Priory. On seeing French he pulled up. French told him of the interview he had just had.

'She came to me about that,' Headley answered. 'Thinks there must have been some other cause than that we suppose.' To French he seemed slightly dissatisfied.

'You didn't find anything to suggest another cause?'

'I didn't, and that's a fact. I didn't find anything to suggest any cause.' He hesitated; then went on: 'Tell you what, Mr French. Now you're here, what about stepping up with me and having a look round. Quite unofficial, you know. Constable and I were just saying in the study that if it had been murder we'd have been asking you officially. I wonder, sir, if you'd be so good?'

French thought of his holiday. Then he thought of the sergeant's boat and the sergeant's trouble to give him a good time. The man seemed really anxious that he should go. Unofficially, of course, he could, and reluctantly he agreed.

An hour later the two then were walking up the Priory Drive. The grounds were well kept, and everywhere there were evidences of wealth. From the terrace, with its grass sward level as a billiard table, there was a fine view out over the sea. The house was of moderate size, but luxuriously fitted, with two staircases and bathrooms to every bed-room. The sergeant led the way to the study.

'This,' he said, locking the door behind them, 'is where the affair happened. The body has, of course, been taken upstairs.'

French stood looking round him. The room was of fair size, with a large bow window in one of the longer walls. Two panes of this bow were carried down to form a french window, which gave on the lawn at the side of the house. In the bow, facing outwards, stood a large flat-topped writing desk, with a revolving chair. The remaining furniture was plain, but good. A pleasant, leisurely room with a peaceful air far removed from tragedy.

'The deceased was sitting there in the chair before his desk,' Sergeant Headley went on. 'His body had fallen forward and his head was lying on the desk. His right arm was hanging down and in the hand he was grasping the revolver. He was shot in the right temple and the blood had run on the desk. Otherwise there was nothing abnormal either about him or anything else in the room. Death was instantaneous.'

French could picture the scene, particularly as an ugly stain on the desk showed where the head had lain.

'Where's the gun?' he asked.

The sergeant opened a drawer in the desk. 'Here,' he answered, lifting out a small revolver.

It was a remarkable little weapon, and French examined it curiously. Silver-mounted and delicately chased, it was of small bore and light weight. It was loaded in five of its six chambers, with an empty shell-case in the sixth.

'Nice little gun, that,' said French. 'Where did he get it?'

Headley opened another drawer and withdrew a small morocco-covered case.

'He'd had it for years – without a licence – and he kept it in this case. As you see, the case was made for two, but there appears to have been only one in it. I take it they were duelling pistols.'

'Looks like it. Did you inquire about the second one?'

'No one had seen it. No one knew of the existence of this one except Lady Goodliffe, and she had never seen more than one in the case.'

French nodded. 'Did you get the bullet?'

'Yes, the doctor extracted it.'

'And it fitted the gun, I suppose I need scarcely ask?'

'It fitted the gun all right. You'll notice it's a special size, small for a revolver.'

'I see that. Well, that's the position of the deceased. What evidence did you get from the household?'

'The household consists, or rather consisted, of Sir Charles and Lady Goodliffe, the butler John, and two maids, Jennie and Peters. There is also a chauffeur, but he lives in the village and had gone home. As nearly as the others could remember, it was just after half past ten when the shot was heard. Jennie and the butler were in the kitchen, which is close by, and they came running at once to the hall and knocked at this door. The butler tried to open it and found it locked. Mrs Peters had gone to bed. Lady Goodliffe had also gone to bed, and Jennie ran up for her. But on the stairs she met her hurrying down in a dressing-gown. Lady Goodliffe had been practically in bed when she heard the shot. She also tried the study door, calling her husband's name, but there was no reply. Then she shouted to try the French window, and they all ran out of the hall door and round here. The window was closed, but unlocked, and they came in. The deceased was lying where I have described. They were naturally greatly upset, but they seem to have kept their heads. They unlocked this door and came out into the hall and rang up Dr Browne and the station. The doctor and I arrived about the same time, but he could do nothing. I got these particulars, and

I've fixed up with the Coroner for tomorrow morning for the inquest.'

'Who was the last person to see the deceased alive?'

'A nephew, a Mr Sholto Goodliffe, a man of about thirty. He lives in a small house on the estate with a couple of servants, and acted as Sir Charles's secretary. Pretty much of a sinecure, I should think. Mr Sholto frequently dined at the Priory, and he did so on the evening in question. After dinner the three of them, Sir Charles, Lady Goodliffe and Mr Sholto, sat here. About ten Lady Goodliffe, who was suffering from a headache, went to bed. It was half an hour later that the shot was heard.

'I've seen Mr Sholto, and he says that he left the house a few minutes after Lady Goodliffe went upstairs. He let himself out by the French window, for, as it was a warm night, he had neither coat nor hat with him. That was about ten-fifteen. He is sure of the time because he looked at his watch on reaching his own house and it was then just ten-twenty.'

'What about the deceased's manner?'

'He was depressed, but not more so than often before. He was dyspeptic, and it affected his mind. But there's evidence to show that whatever upset him didn't upset him till after Mr Sholto left.'

'That's interesting. What is it?'

'He had been writing a letter, and he had broken off in the middle of a sentence. And the letter was about a visit he intended to pay in London.'

French was pleased. He thought the sergeant had done well. He seemed to have looked for everything and he certainly knew his facts.

'Then what's your theory?' he asked, curious to hear what the man would say.

Headley moved uneasily. 'That's not so simple, Mr French.' He put his head on one side and half closed his eyes. 'What about his having had a visitor?'

'Well, what about it?'

'I look at it this way, sir.' He became very confidential. 'I've been making inquiries about that rumour I was telling you of, and I'm told it's a true bill about the wife. She's been running about with Mr Pettigrew a deal more than was wise. What if Pettigrew had come up to have a talk about it? He would have seen through the window that the old man was alone.'

'And then?'

'Why, that Sir Charles saw that he had lost his wife. He was depressed to start with, and the realization might have given him a sudden impulse to end it all. Pettigrew might have been there when it happened and slipped away without saying anything, or he might have left before it.'

'You didn't suspect Pettigrew of murdering him?'

'Couldn't have, sir, as you know. You can't close a dead man's hand on the gun, and you can't shoot him with it if he's holding it himself, not without his resisting, anyway, and there was no resistance here.'

'You've no proof of all this theory about Pettigrew?'

'It's guesswork pure and simple,' Headley admitted. 'I'm only mentioning it to you in confidence. I may be quite wrong.'

French nodded. Really the sergeant had done very well. Yet there was always danger in jumping to conclusions. He thought for a few moments, then went on slowly:

'Well, sergeant, that's all very good. But do you know what I'd do if I were in your place?'

Headley looked his question.

'I'll tell you. I'd take a whole lot more trouble. For one thing, I'd look round for fingerprints and check any I found with the dead man's. I'd try the gun and the case and the key and the door handles and anything else I could think of. I'd have a further general look round for anything I could find. I'd have the score markings on the bullet and the gun checked up. I'd find out if Pettigrew was there – if I could. All those things should be done whether you expect to find anything or not. It's the proper routine, and if you do it it keeps you straight whatever happens.'

Headley looked puzzled. Apparently he was wondering whether or not French was pulling his leg. Why should he spend a lot of time making useless inquiries when there was so much that had to be done before the inquest? French watched with some curiosity, then as soon as he could do so without hurting the man's feelings, he excused himself. He was bored with the whole affair. Besides there was the question of the busman's holiday.

All the same, he could not get the affair entirely out of his mind. As he tramped along over the heather-covered cliffs that afternoon – Mrs French had gone to tea with an acquaintance – it forced its way back into his thoughts.

Oh well, it was not his case and he need not worry. All the same…Headley was a good fellow. He must not be allowed to make any mistake. French decided that he would stroll up to the Priory next morning and have another word with him before the inquest.

★   ★   ★

But Headley himself took the initiative. As French and his wife were breakfasting next morning a whirlwind was announced. It was the staid and portly sergeant, his eyes bursting from his head with excitement and his voice breathless as if he had run to the cottage.

'Mr French, sir,' he cried, scarcely noticing Mrs French's presence, 'the friction marks on that bullet and on the barrel are different; they don't coincide! The bullet was never fired out of that gun at all!'

'Ah,' said French, looking up with interest, 'I thought it mightn't have been. That's why I advised you to get a microscopic test made.'

'But – 'The sergeant subsided on to the nearest chair and stared helplessly. 'I don't understand,' he gasped. 'There was the revolver in the man's hand with one shell discharged, and there was the bullet in his head. And there was no other gun and no other bullet. I don't see – '

French chuckled. 'Here,' he said, 'pull that chair in to the table and have a cup of coffee and a pipe. That'll cool you down and you can start and think.'

'But the inquest's at eleven o'clock.'

'Bless us all, what if it is? It's only nine now. Plenty of time. Pour him out a cup, mother.'

The sergeant protested splutteringly, then did as he was told. Suitably drugged by coffee and tobacco, he became once more a normal individual. French then opened the discussion.

'You told me yesterday that you thought Sir Charles had a visitor just before the tragedy, and gave a neat little demonstration to support your theory. It was so neat that I took it as proof. It was obvious that while he was writing his letter the deceased had not intended to commit suicide, and only a visitor could have produced in the time such a tremendous revulsion of feeling."

The sergeant nodded.

'Now,' French went on, 'if that visitor, instead of provoking the deceased to suicide, had murdered him, Sir Charles' comparatively normal manner, his interest in his visit to town, and his breaking off in the middle of a sentence are at once explained.'

'That's true, sir. But the gun grasped in the hand?'

'Quite so – but,' French became very impressive, 'what if there were two guns?'

The sergeant started. 'Two guns? But there weren't two.'

'There were once; the case proves that. It doesn't follow that they were both kept in the case. Suppose your visitor arrives and they quarrel over the lady as you suggested. Suppose the visitor says: "Look here, Sir Charles, let's settle it in the old-fashioned way, once and for all. You told me you had a pair of duelling pistols. Let's have 'em out and use them." Sir Charles agrees and gets the guns from wherever they were kept. Each takes one, but before they have got into position the visitor shoots Sir Charles. He at once decamps with the other gun and is gone before the servants can get in. What about something like that happening, Headley?'

The sergeant was visibly impressed. With muttered imprecations he admitted that it might well have taken place.

'It's as much of a guess as your own,' French concluded, 'but it's a theory to start you with. At all events, your immediate problem is solved. You must have an adjournment. And if you take my advice you won't let the reason leak out.'

'I'll put the Coroner wise, sir. Are you coming to the inquest?'

'Well, who do you take me for?' French retorted. 'Has it occurred to you that I'm supposed to be on holiday?'

★   ★   ★

That afternoon French was once again sitting outside the cottage when Headley appeared on his way back to the Priory. As before, he stopped to talk.

'The inquest passed off as easy as butter,' he declared. 'That Coroner is a downy bird. Said the police weren't satisfied as to motive and he would adjourn for a fortnight. No suspicion raised anywhere.' He hesitated and hung about for a moment on one foot. 'I suppose, Mr French, you couldn't see your way to have another look round up there, unofficially, of course? I don't mind confessing I'm a bit at sea with this new development. The Super's been on the job, but he's gone back without saying anything.'

French considered. Though it was his holiday, the affair had taken possession of his mind and he knew he would not be happy till it was settled. He shrugged good-humouredly.

'Anything for a quiet life,' he said, and they fell into step.

'You got no fingerprints, I suppose?' he went on.

Headley grinned sheepishly. 'No, sir. I'm afraid everything was covered with my own. But I've got a good deal of other stuff. First, I found out that Pettigrew had an alibi. It happens that he makes a hobby of wood-carving, and he was working at it in his workshop at the time.'

'How do you know that?'

'His statement is corroborated by the servants. There are three – a man and his wife, butler and cook, and a housemaid. Pettigrew went to the workshop after dinner, as he often did. It's a room beside the study that he's fitted up. There's a bell from it to the kitchen, and about ten he rang. He wanted some whisky, and the butler took it in. He was then chipping away, roughing something out of a big block with his mallet and chisel. He stayed working at it till eleven, when he came in and his man saw him again going to bed.'

'That proves he was there at ten and eleven. But how do you know about the hour between?'

'They heard him, all three of them. He was tapping away all the time. They're quite sure it was his hammering and not any other noise, because that hitting with a wooden mallet has a special unmistakable sound that they'd often heard before and knew well. So my first idea was wrong. Pettigrew's out of it.'

'That leaves you in the air?'

'No. I've got something better.' The sergeant became partly impressive and partly triumphant. 'I've found out that Mr Sholto Goodliffe is Sir Charles' heir, that he's hard up, and that he wants to marry.'

French looked at him sharply. 'Oh, you have, have you? What was the old man worth?'

'A cool hundred thousand, so they tell me.'

'A hundred thousand? There's motive there all right. And has this Sholto no alibi?'

'He put up what I told you; that he got home at ten-twenty. But, of course, that's no alibi. He can't prove it.'

'But do you think he'd commit a murder like that without attempting some kind of alibi?'

'Yes, sir, I do. A manufactured alibi is worse than none at all, and I expect he knew it. I think he was banking on the death being taken for suicide. And good enough too: only for you it would have been. All the same, I've no proof against him.'

'Well,' said French, 'I think there's a possibility that you may get your proof. We may take it that the murderer kills Sir Charles with that second revolver and leaves at once by the window. Now, the revolver's going to embarrass him. He daren't be taken with it on him. He would therefore want to get rid of it as soon as possible. How would he do it?'

The sergeant shook his head.

'I suggest,' French went on, 'that he hid it at the first possible moment, somewhere close by. Let's make a search, at all events.'

Headley was only too ready to try anything, and they set to work.

It appeared unlikely that there would have been time to hide the weapon in the study, so after a quick look in the more obvious places, they moved out through the window. Some steps led down to a path which ran from the drive in front, past the window, and round the corner of the house to an entrance in the rear. They began with this path and the area adjoining.

Close to the back door a barrel supported on wooden blocks screened by plants took the water from a downspout. A barrel seemed a likely place, at least for temporary concealment. French moved over to look in.

'Hullo!' he said before reaching it. 'How did that get broken?'

He pointed to a tiny sprig of one of the plants at its base, which showed drooping and withered. Then he stooped down, and pushing his hand past the plant and beneath the barrel, felt about behind its supporting blocks.

'Ah,' he said in a low tone, 'not so dusty this. Hush, don't say anything.'

Headley, looking over his shoulder, saw that he was grasping a revolver the companion of the one found in Sir Charles' hand.

But French did not withdraw the weapon. Instead he pushed it back where he had found it, replaced the foliage, and carefully rubbed out the marks of their footprints.

'Come back to the study,' he went on. 'I expected we'd find that somewhere there.'

The sergeant's eyes once more grew round. 'Expected it?' he stammered. 'I don't know how – '

'No, sergeant,' French interrupted, 'you've not done badly so far. Do a little better while you're at it. Think it out for yourself. You've everything you want to give you the truth.' He paused for a moment, then went on: 'But I'll tell you what you still haven't got, and that is proof against the murderer. Do you see now how you can get it?'

Headley, obviously out of his depth, shook his head.

French could not help smiling at his expression. 'Then,' he said, 'I'll tell you. You've no doubt been troubled with reporters?'

'I've been longing all day to shift them with a stick of dynamite,' the sergeant answered in heartfelt tones.

'Well, they're going to return good for evil. They're going to put the murderer into your hands. Now listen carefully. Go and tell them that the police have formed the theory, so far unproven – so far unproven, mind you – that the deceased did not commit suicide, but was murdered; that he was not shot by the pistol in his hand, but by an exactly similar one; that they believe this second pistol must have been hidden near the scene of the crime and that on the following morning a great search for it is to begin. Say that if the police can find it it will prove their theory and give them information which will unquestionably lead to the murderer. Let them see you are really anxious to find the pistol, but are only hoping against hope that it may exist. See the idea?'

A slow smile spread over Headley's somewhat heavy countenance. 'I've got you, sir, at last. I never would have thought of it. We'll have it in all the morning papers. There's no need to do any more. Sholto'll see it all right. I suppose, all the same, we should watch tonight?'

'Yes, put a couple of men on, but you and I will wait till the next night.'

The morning papers had a story which reflected credit on the efforts of Headley and the reporters. It began by saying that the police, while admitting they had a clue, were exceedingly reticent as to its nature. In spite of this reticence, however, the papers' special correspondent had been able to learn the truth. Then followed the yarn about the revolver, given ostensibly with all reserve, but really in a most convincing manner. French smiled as he read it. He believed it would accomplish its design.

All that day the police found it necessary to conduct their search in the Priory grounds, one or other being in sight of the barrel during the entire time. When they left, French, Headley and a couple of men remained behind, secreted in a convenient shrubbery. With the prevision of a long vigil they settled down to wait.

Their misgivings were justified. Eight, nine, ten and eleven passed, and still there was no sign. The lights in the house went out. It grew colder and the breeze took on an edge. There was no moon, but it was clear and the stars gave a fair light. Save for the faint wash of the waves on the shore, it was very silent. French, cramped behind his bush, would have given a good deal for a smoke. He thought whimsically what a fool he was, putting up with all this discomfort for someone else's case! And yet he knew he wouldn't be satisfied not to be here.

Twelve struck on the village clock; then, after an eternity, one. French began to get sleepy. Curse it, why hadn't he brought a thermos with some coffee to keep him awake? He could remember having kept many a long vigil, but never once had he remembered to take coffee. Well, it would be a useful hint for the future.

Hist! What was that?

A shadow was approaching from the back of the house. It floated along like a more densely black smudge against the lesser black of the background. It moved to the barrel. It stooped down. In a moment it raised itself upright. It began to move away...

This last movement was the signal. Swiftly and silently French began to press forward. The figure stopped as if in hesitation. Then it saw French. It gave a strangled scream and fled in the opposite direction – into the arms of Sergeant Headley, whose huge bulk loomed up like a mountain before it. In a moment French was beside him. He saw a hand turning the revolver towards the sergeant's head. He snatched the weapon aside as the flame spurted from the muzzle. There was a gasp and then a thin despairing cry – in a woman's voice. They were holding Lady Goodliffe.

★   ★   ★

The sergeant was one huge note of interrogation as he sat in French's room next morning. 'But how, sir, did you know?' he kept on repeating.

'I didn't know,' French returned, handing over his pouch, 'but I suspected. And you should have suspected, too. I'll tell you, sergeant.'

He sat forward and checked his points off on his fingers.

As we've seen, the act that Sir Charles was not killed by the gun in his hand proved there was a second one of the same size in existence. Now, it was difficult to believe that only one of those guns should have been kept in their case. Why not both? To keep them together would have been the natural thing. When, therefore, Lady Goodliffe said that only one was there, the question arose, had she a reason for this statement?

'Obviously, Sir Charles could have been shot with the second gun, and if he had been, the murderer would have had an extremely strong reason for denying its existence. Was Lady Goodliffe, then, the murderer?

'I had reached this point when I asked you to get the bullet scoring checked. The result proved it was murder, and at once my idea about Lady Goodliffe recurred to me. I had, of course, noted that she had an adequate motive for the crime. If she were in love with Pettigrew, there it was at once. With Sir Charles' religious beliefs, it was unlikely he'd give her a divorce. But if Sir Charles were dead her path was clear.'

'I saw that, sir.'

'Of course you did, but you didn't follow it up. Very well; so much for motive. Incidentally, I may say that I believe Lady Goodliffe had the necessary character also. When she came to me she seemed much upset, but even then it was all about herself, not her husband. She wasn't sorry for his death.

'I assumed her guilt to see where it would lead, and at once I saw how she could have acted. She would have watched for Sholto leaving and then gone down again to the study. She would have got her husband to pick up one of the guns by some trick; perhaps by saying she had found it on the hall table and asking was it one of his? She would, of course, have fired a shot out of it beforehand. He would pick it up and at the same moment she would shoot him through the temple with the other gun. She would rush to the door and lock it, then hurry out by the window and round to the back door, dropping the gun into her pre-arranged hiding place as she ran. She could not, of course, have put this gun in the case, as there would be no time to clean it. She would enter by the back door, which she would have left unlocked, run up the back stairs, slip on a dressing-gown, and run down the front stairs. I thought all that would be possible, but of course I still did not know if it was true.'

The sergeant seemed overcome with admiration.

'To test the theory, I looked for the gun along the route the lady must have traversed, if guilty. And when we found it, where no outsider would have passed, note you, I felt my theory was the truth. Still we had no proof. Then I saw how we might get it. If the second gun were found, the lady would see that the position of the hiding place would give her away. She would be forced to get it out of that. She tried to do so and so sealed her fate.'

'I've been a fool, Mr French, but there's still one thing I don't understand. If she was guilty, why did she take the risk of asking you to look into the case?'

'No doubt she thought it would divert any possible suspicion, and no doubt also she thought her scheme was so good that it couldn't be found out. But, by the way, didn't you say something in the study about calling me in if it proved to be murder?'

'Yes, we discussed that.'

'There you are, then. I expect she was listening and partially overheard you. She thought you suspected and were going to call me in, and she determined to be beforehand and so divert suspicion from herself. What?…That's all right, sergeant. It's your case. I don't appear.'

★   ★   ★

Taken as it were in the act, there was no defence, and before the end the unhappy woman made a statement which showed that French's theory was substantially correct.

THE LANDING TICKET

'Anything on this afternoon?' asked Curle's colleague, the cashier, as they reached the office door at one o'clock on a damp and dismal Saturday afternoon in early January.

Curle shrugged. 'Got to meet the niece and nephew at Liverpool Street and take them to the movies, worse luck,' he answered. 'Hate the films myself.'

'Virtue'll be its own reward,' the cashier consoled him as he turned west, while Curle, with a smile, continued on his usual way towards the Tube station at the Bank.

Masterman Curle was accountant in the head office of the London and Grimsby, one of the largest and most prosperous insurance companies in the country. He was a very able man and it was a correspondingly well-paid job. Unmarried and living alone in rooms, he ought to have had all the money he wanted. But his tastes were extravagant, and for years he had been short of cash.

As his colleague turned away and Curle found himself alone his expression changed. The smile was as if it were wiped from his face, and a look of keenest anxiety took its place. For a moment he was an old and haggard man. Then, with an obvious effort, he pulled himself together and his features regained the rather strained look of good humour they had previously borne.

But he did not act as if he were looking for his nephew and niece. He was not, in fact, for no such persons existed. Instead of continuing towards the Bank, he turned south to

Cannon Street. There he took a District train to Victoria. At the Pillar Café he ate a hurried lunch. Though at Cook's he had already bought a first return to Paris, he now took another ticket, a second single, also for Paris. Then he retrieved a suitcase which he had left on the previous evening in the cloakroom. Finally, he found an inconspicuous position near the barrier of No. 1 Platform from which the 2 p.m. Continental Boat Express was shortly due to start.

Presently he saw the man for whom he was watching, a stout good-humoured looking fellow in a heavy overcoat. The man did not notice Curle and in due course passed through the barrier. After a few seconds Curle did the same. He watched his quarry enter a first-class carriage and, again after a short delay, followed him in. Save for the man, the compartment was empty. Curle scarcely glanced at him, busying himself in lifting his suitcase to the rack.

'Hullo, Curle,' the man said promptly. 'This is a surprise. You crossing?'

Curle, who was quite a good actor, allowed his features to express with clarity his emotions. First he 'registered' surprise and dismay, which he quickly changed to an embarrassed pleasure.

'Hullo, Lucas,' he returned a little breathlessly. 'This certainly is a surprise to me. But it shouldn't have been, for I remember now you said you were crossing this afternoon. Yes, I'm going, too. Job for the firm in Paris.'

'Oh, well, that's not so bad. I shall have someone to talk to now.'

'Yes, I'm glad too,' Curle agreed, with more truth than was apparent on the surface. For the fact was that the presence of Lucas was an essential condition for the carrying out of the scheme which Curle had in hand.

He was crossing to Paris, yes. But not on a job for his firm. Quite the reverse, in fact. For Curle was an absconding thief, and he had stolen some £20,000 of his firm's money. This journey represented the culmination of his plan, and if he could carry it through successfully he would feel safe to enjoy the fruits of his crime.

The plan had been carefully thought out. More than a year previously he had accidentally discovered a weak spot in his firm's financial system. He had 'borrowed' to get himself out of a temporary difficulty. He knew that in a week he would be able to repay the money, as his next month's salary would then be due. He had repaid it and no one had suspected what had happened. The firm's annual audit occurred shortly after and nothing had come out.

Then Curle fell into temptation. His scheme had succeeded on a small scale: would it not do so equally on a large? If he were able to get away with £30, why not with £30,000? He could not pass an audit undiscovered but he had a year till the next audit, and in a year what might he not do?

For a time he resisted the temptation. Then he grew short of money again. For the second time he 'borrowed.' He did not intend to take much, only enough to get him out of his immediate difficulty. But this time, instead of replacing the sum from his next month's salary, he took more...Presently he found himself hopelessly involved.

Then temptation smote him with redoubled force. By developing his plan he could get money, not merely for present relief, but to keep him in moderate luxury for the rest of his life. Owing to his position as accountant he could put through cooked weekly statements. These would pass – until next year's audit. By that time he would have made his pile and cleared out.

Curle fell before the temptation. He worked out his scheme with immense concentration, and so far had carried it out with equal care.

It was divided into three main parts. First, there was the actual getting of the money with, as its most difficult phase, the changing of it into pound notes, which he could carry away and which could not be traced. Next, there was the provision of an indication that all the money had been spent, and that, therefore, an attempt to recover it would be useless. This must look like an oversight on his part, and he did it by leaving in a notebook, dropped in behind the books on his shelves, the names of horses which had failed to win in the more important races, with large sums jotted down after each. Thirdly, there was the arranging of a hiding place to which he could retreat till the hue and cry, should such arise, had died down.

To act in this last he had prepared a simple disguise: internal heels in his shoes to add an inch to his height; padded underclothes, to make him burly instead of thin; dark horn spectacles of plain glass; a forward-poking, shoulder-swinging way of walking instead of his usual steady and erect carriage; untidy sports clothes instead of a neat office suit: and finally, small pads of rubber in his cheeks to alter the shape of his face. In his ordinary clothes he had gone several times to Portsmouth, changed to his disguise in various lavatories, and then, crossing to Gosport, had rented rooms in a secluded district on the outskirts of the town. He had explained that he was a novelist and wanted a quiet place to work. He had stayed on occasional nights and weekends, saying he would be coming permanently early in January.

He was satisfied that this retreat was entirely unsuspected. It was true that Walker, one of the clerks in the office who lived at Guildford, had seen him more than once in the train, but he explained that he had been with a hypothetical married sister in Ryde.

Up to the present the whole scheme had worked magnificently. Now this journey he was taking to France was its last stage. If he could complete it satisfactorily he would be secure for the remainder of his days.

He had chosen this afternoon, firstly, because his audit was coming very close and, secondly, because his plan depended on his finding some acquaintance who was going to Paris, and his neighbour, Lucas, had mentioned that he was going on this day. Saturday, indeed, was the most suitable day for him, but, if necessary, he would have gone on another day, advising the office that he was unwell.

Lucas was a talkative man, and they chatted most of the way to Dover. During the journey Curle was careful to give the impression that he had a weight on his mind. Deliberately he was absent-minded and 'queer'. Under the circumstances the effect was easy to achieve, as he had only to allow his real fears to find expression in his manner.

At Dover they went together through the British passport examination and aboard the *Ashford*. The damp of Town had here changed to a driving rain, and a gusty wind was blowing up Channel. From the train the sea had looked rough, and now through the opening between the pier-heads they got a glimpse of grey-capped waves driving north. It was not going to be a pleasant crossing. All the better for Curle. He was never sick, and the deck would be deserted, as he had hoped.

Having secured seats on the covered main deck, the two men went aft for the French passport examination. As everyone knows, this takes place on these boats immediately after leaving. The passports are stamped and returned to the holders with passport landing tickets. Without one of these, no one can go ashore in France.

The examination was the first point of danger for Curle: he must not allow anyone to know that he had obtained a landing ticket. When, therefore, they were near the head of the queue he suddenly left his place, saying, 'Oh, there's Mitford! I must speak to him.' He hurried away out of Lucas' sight, then, slipping into an unoccupied private cabin, he watched till he saw Lucas go past. After giving him time to get well away, Curle returned to the passport queue and in due course obtained his landing ticket.

He hastened after Lucas. 'That was a man,' he explained, 'whom I haven't seen for years. He's crossing second-class, but we're to meet in Paris. By Jove, we're going to catch it!'

Opportunely for Curle, the *Ashford* at that moment gave a corkscrew plunge which caused Lucas's book to slide off his knee. By the time it was retrieved the question of Mitford and passport landing tickets had been forgotten.

Lucas was as good a sailor as Curle, and the amount of movement in the ship was unlikely to cause either serious discomfort. They chatted until presently the purser's officer came round to check their tickets. Curle handed him the first return he had bought at Cook's, and which, of course, he had also used in the train. It was a little book, and the officer tore out a page and returned the book with a travel landing ticket. By the system in force no passenger could land without showing two landing tickets, representing respectively that the passport was in order and the fare paid.

At once it became time for the next step in Curle's scheme. With a muttered apology he left Lucas and went down the alleyway. In a lavatory he put on part of his disguise, which he had secreted in the pockets of his reversible coat. Then he went to the second-class, and when the purser's officer came round he handed up the second-class ticket he had bought at Victoria – also a book from which a page was torn – and for it obtained a second landing ticket. Then in another lavatory he changed back to his normal garb and rejoined Lucas.

The waves had grown steeper as they got further from land, and the *Ashford* was pitching and rolling uncomfortably. Dull thuds sounded forward as seas hit her bow, and after each she quivered, as if gently shaking herself free of the water. The howl of the wind through the deck fittings penetrated to where the two men sat, and a tumbled grey and slate sea swam up and down before the side windows, alternately blocking out half the sky and sinking out of sight. Both in their secret hearts wished they were ashore.

For half an hour or more they sat chatting desultorily. Then, when they were close to the French side, Curle told himself that the great moment of his scheme had arrived. To prepare for it he had allowed his manner to become increasingly perturbed. He had simulated fits of absentmindedness, from which he had recovered with a start. Now he got up and, leaving his suitcase, muffler, book and umbrella with Lucas, he murmured that he was not feeling too well, and was going on deck for a little air.

Lucas' interest in what was taking place had by this time considerably dwindled, and he replied by a short nod. Curle staggered away to the stairs and jerkily mounted.

He was not really sick, however, and directly he was out of sight of Lucas he carried on with his plan. Once again he put on his disguise in a lavatory and returned to the second-class. They were by this time inside the Calais moles, and he had scarcely mingled with the passengers when they drew in towards the wharf.

Curle went ashore in the densest crowd of people he could find. He gave up his passport landing ticket and the fare landing ticket he had received in the second-class, carrying that he had obtained for his first-class ticket in his pocket. He hastened to a second-class carriage as near the engine of the Paris train as possible. At Paris he left the Gare du Nord with the earliest passengers.

He stayed the night at a small hotel and next day crossed back to England by Dieppe and Newhaven, of course, taking a fresh ticket. Having left the service at Newhaven, he went by bus to Brighton. In Brighton he put on his full disguise, recovering a suitcase he had previously left at the station cloakroom. By evening he had reached his rooms at Gosport.

There he settled down to write. He had brought with him a copy of an old book, *This Mortal Coil*, by Grant Allen, and every day he copied out so many pages, as proof to his landlady of his bona fides. He went out only after dark and for a time spoke to no one.

But soon he felt he must have *some* human intercourse if he were not to go mad. He began in the evenings to visit a nearby public house. Only working-class people attended, and with them he thought he would be safe. Then, after a time, he would complete his plan. He would simulate illness, and while in bed would grow a beard and moustache. With these as a further disguise he would move to a new lodging in some distant place, where at last he would be safe.

II

That something serious was weighing upon Curle's mind, Lucas was sure from the first moment he met him. He was a man whom Lucas did not greatly admire, but at the golf club he had found him good company and for that reason had asked him to his house. Curle had proved entertaining, and as Mrs Lucas and the children had liked him, the invitation had on several occasions been repeated. The two men, however, had never become more than acquaintances.

Some five minutes after Curle had gone on deck the *Ashford* passed in between the twin moles at Calais, at once exchanging her corkscrew twisting for a steadier and more dignified gait. Lucas thanked his gods that the crossing was so well over. He collected his things and began to realize that he had missed his tea.

Curle's belongings were on the seat beside him, and Lucas wished the man would come back so that he could go on deck for a breath of fresh air. But there was no sign of Curle.

They sidled up to the wharf and moored. The gangways were put aboard and the passengers began to stream down them. Still the man didn't turn up.

'Curse the fellow!' thought Lucas. 'Here I am in charge of his things, and if he doesn't look sharp, I'll not get a corner seat in the train.'

It was of course no business of his to look after Curle's gear, but Lucas at heart was a kindly man, and if Curle were unwell or in trouble he didn't wish to seem to desert him. Finally he compromised. He called a steward, told him the circumstances, and put him in charge of the stuff. Then he went ashore and climbed into the train.

There was the usual delay in starting, but when the time was almost up the steward appeared, looking along the train. He saw Lucas and beckoned him into the corridor.

'That gentleman, sir, that you spoke to me about,' he said, 'he's disappeared. He never came back and we don't think he went ashore. There's bound to be an inquiry, and the purser would be obliged if you'd kindly come back to the boat and make a statement. You can get another train in half an hour.'

Lucas was horrified. 'Good God!' he exclaimed. 'Disappeared! I'll go, of course. Help me with my things.'

'Sorry to bring you back, sir,' the purser apologized when Lucas was seated in his cabin, 'but it doesn't look too well about this gentleman. May I ask if he's a friend of yours?'

'He's an acquaintance,' Lucas replied; 'he lives near me. What exactly has happened?'

'That's just what we're trying to find out. I should be obliged if you'd tell me anything about him that you can.'

'Of course.' Lucas gave first his own name and address, then Curle's, Curle's business, that he lived alone and other details.

'You travelled over with him?'

'Yes, we met by chance at Victoria.'

'Was Mr Curle quite normal in his manner?'

'Well, he was not,' Lucas admitted. 'I was a good deal struck by his restlessness and preoccupation. He certainly seemed to have something on his mind.'

The purser nodded. 'I'm afraid it looks badly. Can you – ' he hesitated, then went on: 'Is there any reason to make you fear – suicide?'

'No,' Lucas returned promptly, 'none whatever. I shouldn't believe it for a moment. But why jump to such a conclusion? How do you know he didn't go ashore?'

'I'll tell you, sir. 175 tickets were collected from the passengers and 175 landing tickets were given out against them. But only 174 were recovered at the gangway. The holder of that 175th ticket didn't go ashore. Therefore he should be on board. But no passengers remain on board. Therefore – You see, sir?'

Lucas was greatly shocked and troubled. What could have been weighing so heavily on Curle's mind to have led him to so desperate a remedy? Suicide presupposed a quite intolerable situation. Dreadful! Very much upset, Lucas went on to Paris.

In the meantime events moved as they normally do move in such unhappy circumstances. The captain was informed, then the Southern agents, and then the police. Inquiries were made in London, at Curle's rooms, from the manager of the London and Grimsby, from those of the missing man's friends who could be found.

But until Monday afternoon nothing further was learnt which threw any real light on the affair. Shortly after lunch an excited auditor sought Mr Matheson, the manager of the insurance company. He was very distressed to say it, but there was no doubt that heavy defalcations had taken place. The books had been falsified with immense skill, and only a man in the accountant's position could have done it.

Acting more or less with the police, the Company's own private detective went very carefully into the affair. He reported that the money had been stolen by Curle and lost in betting on horses, and that when the man found the audit approaching and knew that discovery was certain, he had committed suicide. Curle had no possessions of value, and nothing could be done in the matter except to write the money off as a total loss.

III

But Matheson was far from satisfied with this report. He knew Curle and he did not think such an action was in conformity with his character. He had not, of course, suspected that his accountant was a thief, but he had known him to be selfish and self-seeking. Much too hard-headed to waste good money in gambling, he thought, and much too fond of himself to commit suicide.

And yet the evidence seemed overwhelming. These steamer people had a pretty complete check on their passengers – they had to in order to protect themselves against fraud. There could be little doubt that one person fewer had gone ashore at Calais than had embarked at Dover. And of that there could only be one explanation.

However, £20,000 was £20,000. Matheson thought the situation over for half an hour, then he took a taxi to Scotland Yard.

'I admit,' he said to Sir Mortimer Ellison, the Assistant Commissioner, 'that the evidence of Curle's death seems convincing. But I think suicide so unlike his character that I urgently beg that a further investigation be made by a qualified man. The local police I know are good, but it's obvious that they couldn't equal your staff. If necessary, my firm would pay the cost of an inquiry.'

'It's not a question of money,' Sir Mortimer returned, as Matheson had shrewdly suspected before he made his offer. 'It's a question of convincing us that there really is something to investigate.'

'Well,' said Matheson, 'look here,' and he went on to restate his suspicions as strongly as he knew how. At last Sir Mortimer compromised.

'I'll tell you what I'll do,' he decided. 'I'll let a man go into these points you have raised. If they convince him, we'll have the inquiry.'

As a result of this decision Chief Inspector French found himself an hour later at the office of the London and Grimsby. A short discussion with the auditor and officials of the firm served to show him Curle's exact position with the firm and the method of the fraud. He found also that

Matheson's estimate of the man's character was shared by a good number of his associates. French reported that in his opinion there was a case for inquiry. He was at once instructed to proceed.

At first his steps were dictated by routine. After getting all the technical details possible at the office, he went on to find out what he could from the staff as to Curle's spare-time activities. Here, however, he learnt little, though Walker told him about sometimes seeing Curle in the trains between Waterloo and Portsmouth.

Before leaving the office French photographed all the fingerprints he could find on the inside of Curle's safe and private drawers. Then he went on to the man's rooms, and finding the same prints on the desk there, he thought he might assume they were Curle's.

In the rooms he found nothing of interest except the small notebook containing the betting entries. These he checked up in detail, with somewhat suggestive results. He found that all the horses had run on the dates mentioned, and had won or lost as stated. So far the notes seemed perfectly genuine, but from another point of view they were less convincing. All his efforts to trace the actual transactions failed. That he should not find all of them was only to be expected, but that after circularizing all the chief bookmakers he should not get on to even one, did seem remarkable. The fact did not prove anything, but it changed French's vague idea that Curle might be alive, into a definite suspicion.

'It looks as if the fellow had done us after all,' he said to Sergeant Carter when later the two men were *en route* for Dover to interview the staff of the *Ashford*. 'I'm inclined to believe he's hooked it with the cash. But if so, I'm hanged if I can see how he managed it.'

'Perhaps you'll get the tip aboard the boat, sir,' Carter returned optimistically.

The purser explained to French the method of checking the passengers. Anyone might have come on to the boat with one, or a dozen, or no tickets. But no one could leave it without having given up a ticket and obtained a landing card in exchange.

On the trip in question 175 landing tickets had been given. 174 had been collected at the gangway. Some one person therefore came on board who did not go ashore. So much the purser could stand over.

French thought for a moment. Then he asked if there were not similar landing tickets in connection with the passports and if these were also counted.

The purser shrugged. 'Well, now,' he answered, while the suspicion of a wink trembled on his left eyelid, 'it's not for me to say what these Frenchmen do. But I can tell you that they were counted on this trip, for once a question arose about a missing passenger, every check was made. As you'd expect, 174 passport landing tickets were given up.'

'I didn't mean that,' French explained. 'Is it known how many were issued?'

'I believe so,' the purser said, with an inimitable suggestion of scepticism in his manner, 'but you'd better see the Frenchmen themselves. What they told me was that they had a thousand to start with, and there were 826 left in their box. That means they gave out 174. Curle evidently knew he would never land and so didn't bother to get his passport checked.'

Of this French was not so sure, though he remembered that Lucas had not seen Curle at the passport office. Again the point proved nothing, but again it was suggestive.

As French returned to London he puzzled over the problem. If Curle had staged a disappearance, how had he done it? And more fundamentally still, *had* he staged a disappearance? Was there any way of finding out?

Then suddenly French thought he saw what might have been done. Suppose Curle had obtained *two* travel tickets? Suppose he had changed them both for fare landing tickets and had gone ashore on one and destroyed the other?

This, French saw, would meet the case as he knew it. But was it truth or only ingenious theory?

For the whole of that evening he turned the question over in his mind. How was he to find out whether Curle had carried out such a trick? Did the plan contain any intrinsic or fundamental error which, if he applied the right test, would give it away? Again and again he went over its every detail, but always it seemed to him entirely watertight.

'Can't you see your way through it, Carter?' he grumbled. 'What good are you, man? Or,' he added as an afterthought, 'for the matter of that, what good am I either?'

It was not, indeed, till the following day, when he was again discussing the case with Carter, that light suddenly shone into French's mind. Then suddenly he saw there was a fundamental flaw in Curle's scheme, which the man might easily have overlooked. And better still, the question of whether he had seen and guarded against it could easily be settled.

'Bless us all!' French exclaimed. 'A nice pair of idiots we are! All the proof we want is there to be had for the picking up, and we haven't troubled to ask for it. Come along and see what they can do for us at Waterloo.'

To a high official of the Audit Department French stated his business. 'You have a complete record of all the tickets used on that journey?' he went on.

'Yes, we're forced to keep that,' the official returned, 'as the money received for each ticket has to be divided out between our railway service, the steamers, and the Nord Company of France. The collected tickets are returned either here or to Paris and checked up with the sales.'

'Then can you tell me whether all the passengers who crossed on that trip came from London, or whether any joined the service at Dover?'

This took some looking up, but it was presently discovered that none had joined at Dover.

'Then,' said French, trying hard to keep the eagerness out of his voice, 'how many passengers travelled from London to Dover?'

Again there was a delay, and the answer came. 174!

French slapped his thigh with satisfaction. 174, and not 175 passengers had gone aboard at Dover! 174 had landed at Calais. Therefore no one had gone overboard in mid-Channel! Curle was not dead. And it was a hundred chances to one that that £20,000 had never been spent in betting. Curle had made a bad mistake. He had forgotten that he should have carried out the trick with the tickets in the train also. Or more probably, when he had tried to do so, he had found that it was impossible. The collectors pass through the train, checking each person in rotation, and no one could therefore get in front of them unnoticed and give up a second ticket.

French was more than delighted. His test had proved a trump. Here at last was certainty. To find Curle should now be only a matter of routine.

It was obvious that the man would have to lie low somewhere till the case was forgotten. But such a hiding place must be prepared beforehand, as it would be too risky to turn up unexpectedly just at the moment when a man of similar appearance was found to be missing. Previous preparation involved choosing a locality near enough London to enable Curle to visit it while still attending to business.

Of recent visits from town, the only ones of which French had heard were those along the Portsmouth line, mentioned by the Guildford clerk, Walker. Once Walker had travelled with Curle in the 5.50 from Waterloo. This train stopped only at Havant, Fratton and Portsmouth.

The services of the local police in these areas were then enlisted. Laborious inquiries among railway, steamboat and bus staff followed. Hotels and boarding houses were visited, while keepers of 'rooms' were pumped as to their recent lettings. Then suddenly French's growing despondency was changed into delight. At long last he heard of the arrival of the novelist.

That night French followed the man to the Bull and Goat, and by arrangement with the landlord was able to examine his glass. His satisfaction deepened when he found the fingerprints it bore were the same as those he had found on Curle's desk.

When Curle left the inn French and two policemen were waiting for him. His surprise was so great that he submitted quietly to arrest. A search revealed in a suitcase notes for the greater part of the missing money.

'His scheme was perfectly sound,' French said afterwards. 'If only he had given up his second ticket in the train as well as on the boat, his suicide would not have been questioned. And if the thief of the London and Grimsby was known to be dead, the novelist of Gosport would never have been suspected. They all make a slip – if only you can find it.'

THE RAINCOAT

Stephen Horrabin's heart was thumping as he crouched behind the shrubs on the lane passing the private hotel at which he boarded, for he was just about to undertake the most dreadful action of his life, the murder of his chief, Charles Perring.

Of the three partners in the firm of auctioneers, Perring was the senior, a man named Vennor was next, and he, Horrabin, was junior. Very much of a junior the other two made him feel, and he hated them for it. But no doubt in time they would have taken him more into their confidence, had he not by his own act turned them into implacable if unconscious enemies. He had in fact stolen a large sum from the firm and at the audit, now nearly due, the affair must inevitably come out. He knew that neither would hesitate to prosecute.

He felt he could not face prison and the loss and ruin of everything he valued. After agonies of indecision he had chosen the ghastly alternative. He would murder Perring by a method which would involve Vennor. The law then would deal with Vennor. With both of them out of the way he could cover his defalcations and settle down to a happy and law abiding life. Or so he thought.

His scheme was founded on the layout of the area, the outer suburbs of a thriving market town in Berkshire. This lane beside which he was hiding was private. It struck off from the main road some hundred yards back, passed his residential hotel, and after serving some half dozen small houses, petered out into fields. Beside the lane ran the single line of railway terminating in the town, and across it were two other houses. To these a path from the lane over a level crossing made a short cut for foot passengers. In one of them lived Perring, and Horrabin's plan for him was to arrange an accident on the crossing. The second was occupied by two elderly sisters, neither of whom went out at night. The chances of interruption or discovery were therefore practically nil.

Vennor lived in the same residential hotel as Horrabin, but while Vennor had a fine room overlooking the sweep of the valley to the distant hills, Horrabin's was small and restricted in view. Both were bachelors, but Perring was married and had two small children.

While Horrabin still hesitated over his dread purpose, he recalled a discovery he had made some weeks earlier. Trespassing one evening on the railway in search of a rabbit which he had wounded with his airgun, he found himself alongside the Perrings' garden. This was screened from the railway by a belt of trees, but it just happened that he was opposite a small gap in the branches. He was not looking specially, but what he saw through it caused him to stop and stare like a lynx. In the secluded garden were Mrs Perring and Vennor and they were in each other's arms. Perring, he remembered, was in London on business.

Horrabin now realised how profoundly this would affect his scheme. The scheme in itself was good, but it had the fatal flaw that it failed to supply Vennor with a motive. Now that flaw was eliminated. Here was motive enough for any crime. The slightest suspicion of Vennor and the police would quickly unearth so significant a factor.

Now all Horrabin required was opportunity, and this evening he had found it. Perring was taking the chair in the town at a committee meeting of his political party, and Horrabin was certain that Vennor, a member, would be present also. They would walk back together as they always did, Vennor going into the hotel and Perring continuing alone. It was for this that Horrabin was waiting.

He had made careful preparations for the deed. First, seizing his chance, he had gone to the porter's box and taken an impression of Vennor's key, afterwards cutting a copy. When Vennor was out he had slipped into his room and examined his raincoat. This was of a well-known make and during a visit to London he bought one exactly similar. He had marked it with Vennor's name in the same kind of lettering, loosened the buttons to correspond, and kneaded it and dirtied it till it was practically identical with the other. On this evening of the crime, after watching Vennor go down to dinner, he had again slipped into his room and changed the raincoats, taking care to transfer gloves and one or two papers in the pockets. Vennor had gone out wearing the duplicate.

Shortly before the meeting was due to end Horrabin had put on gumboots and Vennor's coat and let himself secretly out of a side door. In the common garage he had dropped into the coat pocket a heavy spanner from Vennor's car. He had walked to a call box, and ringing back to the hotel, had asked in a disguised voice for Vennor. On being told he was out, he had given a message: Would Mr Vennor please call up 3847 at ten that evening and ask for Mr Phillips? The number was that of an hotel in the main street of the town and Phillips was the name a client with whom the firm was in correspondence. It was then that Horrabin had taken up his position behind the shrubs.

The night was raw and overcast, though a quarter moon gave a pallid light. Earlier there had been heavy rain, but this had turned into a fine mist. A chill wind moaned dismally through the trees. Horrabin was shivering, though not from cold. The waiting had got on his nerves and every moment he felt his self-control slipping away. At last stark terror so overwhelmed him that he began to doubt whether he could carry through his terrible enterprise. Then the two expected figures came in sight and with the need for action his nerves steadied.

As they approached he shrank further down behind the shrubs. Their footsteps rang out and then he could hear their voices. They were talking about the meeting and stood for a moment before the hotel.

'Come in for a drink,' he heard Vennor say. But Perring wouldn't. His small daughter was sick and he wanted to get back as soon as possible. 'Another night,' he said as they parted. He strode on his way while Vennor turned into the hotel. Keeping to the grass, Horrabin crept silently after him. On the open lane the man's figure was just visible, but should he look round he would be unlikely to see Horrabin against the bushes.

In due course Perring reached the stile leading to the railway. Horrabin allowed him to cross to the other side, then he ran to the stile, climbed noisily over and shouted, 'Perring! Perring!'

Perring turned and retraced his steps till they met as Horrabin had intended on the actual rails.

'Oh Perring!' Horrabin exclaimed excitedly, 'there's bad news! Just heard there's a fire at the office! Vennor's getting out his car!'

Perring swore and started back towards the lane. This allowed Horrabin to get behind him and he brought the spanner down heavily on his head above the ear. Perring dropped like a stone. Horrabin had struck below the hat, as he wanted to draw blood. A thin trickle did run down and he saw to it that some reached the spanner and the sleeve of Vennor's raincoat.

Horrabin had now become so completely absorbed in his actions that his panic was forgotten. Coolly he arranged the body with the head against the rail, so that the marks of his blow would be obliterated by the engine. Two trains were practically due, one inwards in five minutes, the other out ten minutes later. He had counted on being in time at least for the second. Had the men returned too late for it he would necessarily have postponed his attempt.

He was now careful to mark the raincoat with rust from the rails and oily grit from the ballast. These with the blood should irrevocably seal Vennor's fate. He glanced at his watch. It was ten minutes to ten and he must be back in his room before the hour.

As he regained the lane the first train passed. A desperate haste now consumed him. Four minutes brought him to the hotel, and having wiped his prints off the spanner, he replaced it in Vennor's car. In the ornamental basin of a garden fountain he washed all traces off his gumboots, then by the side door reached his room, again unnoticed. Putting the boots near the fire to dry, he went quickly to a box room opposite Vennor's door and listened.

He had not been there two minutes when he heard ten strike on the hall clock. Immediately afterwards Vennor walked past, no doubt to make the telephone call. The moment the coast was clear Horrabin went into the room and rechanged the raincoats, again remembering the contents of the pockets. Another two minutes and he was back in his own.

Next he must deal with the duplicate raincoat. He had secreted a brick in a drawer, and now he quickly wrapped the coat round it, securing it with string. He opened his door and listened. There was no sound of anyone moving. In his socks he carried the coat along the corridor and up a back stairs to the tank room in the roof. In the tank he sank his parcel as a temporary hiding place till he could dispose of it finally.

His luck held. He returned to his room still unseen, and when he had washed and his boots were dry he breathed more freely. There remained now only the establishment of an alibi.

He felt this should be only suggestive, as too great elaboration would be suspicious. He had previously emptied his bottle of fountain pen ink, and now he went down to the porter and requested a fill for his pen. 'Been doing a job I want to finish,' he explained, 'and my bottle's out.' This established his presence shortly after ten, and he felt that his remark coupled with the fact that he had not passed through the hall during the evening would do the trick.

As he thought over his plan he was satisfied. Vennor had almost certainly been observed leaving the meeting with Perring, and would no doubt be considered the last person to see him alive. No one had observed them part. Vennor's raincoat would be stained with Perring's blood, with rust from the rails and dirt from the ballast. On the other hand, Horrabin's own coat and shoes were dry and there was nothing to suggest that he had left the room.

The motive was equally satisfactory. As Perring was a Catholic and presumably would not stand for a divorce, the intrigue with Mrs Perring would fill the bill. But no one knew of Horrabin's motive. If Vennor were arrested for the crime no one ever would know. Horrabin was safe: safe not only from suspicion of murder, but also from the consequences of his theft.

It was nearly an hour later when a knock came to his door and Vennor looked in. 'Mrs Perring's just rung up,' he declared. 'She seems in a flap about Perring. He's not turned up and she was expecting him home promptly as the daughter's ill.'

Horrabin tried to look annoyed by the interruption. 'Wasn't he at the meeting?' he asked.

'Yes of course he was. We walked back together as usual, and when I came in he went on down the lane.'

'He's called in somewhere else. He'll turn up.'

'It's not like him. Mrs Perring has asked me to go round. I wondered if you'd come? We may have to search for him.'

'Yes of course, if she feels that way.' Horrabin was delighted. Now he would learn at first hand what was going on.

'Just slip a torch into your pocket,' went on Vennor. 'I'll get my coat and we'll go.'

They passed down the lane and climbed the stile on to the railway. Here Horrabin fell back a little. It would be better for Vennor to make the discovery. A moment later there came a startled oath.

'What is it?' Horrabin asked and then swore in his turn.

Vennor was flashing his torch on the body. 'Aye, it's Perring all right!' he cried. 'That incoming train must have got him! I shouldn't have believed it! He was careful about the trains.'

Horrabin was about to reply when a devastating idea shot into his mind. If Vennor stooped to examine the body he would be able to say that he obtained the blood and rust marks in this way.

'Don't touch him!' he exclaimed urgently. 'With those injuries he's certainly dead and the police must see the body before it's moved. Go and tell Mrs Perring and ring up the police from there. I'll wait here till they come.'

Vennor hesitated. 'What a job!' he grumbled. 'But I expect you're right. There are no more trains?'

'No, no. No more tonight.'

To Horrabin the wait in the dark and the cold seemed interminable. Things were not quite so good as he had hoped. Now he would have to give evidence that Vennor appeared surprised at the discovery: if he didn't Vennor would suspect and might give a hint to the police. Then he thought that this was perhaps all to the good. To report in Vennor's favour would divert suspicion from himself.

At long last Vennor reappeared and with him an inspector and sergeant of police. Horrabin knew both slightly. For some moments they bent to examine the remains, then the inspector straightened up.

'From the position of the body it's evident that he was struck by the incoming train. That's due in at 9.50. We'll find out of course if it was on time. Now, Mr Vennor, you tell me you parted from the deceased at the door of your hotel. What time was that?'

'Half past nine, I should say, Inspector, within three or four minutes.'

'In that case he should have been over the crossing before the train. In fact he should have been home when it passed. Now what could have delayed him?'

'I've been wondering that,' Vennor answered. 'Possibly he called at one of the other houses.'

The Inspector considered. 'Slip away to those houses and find out, Raynor,' he told the sergeant. 'We'll wait here for the doctor and ambulance.'

Inspector Hubbard began once more to examine the body, though without touching it. As he did so his face grew longer. Presently he turned to Vennor. 'The Coroner may want a photograph of this. I'd be grateful, Mr Vennor, if you'd go back to the house and ring up for the photographer to come out at once.' He turned to Horrabin as Vennor disappeared. 'You can't be too careful, Mr Horrabin. Omit anything and someone is certain to want it.'

As he spoke he took a piece of chalk from his pocket and began marking on the sleepers the position of the remains. Horrabin watched him with mixed feelings. It was obvious that the man was suspicious. In one way this was all to the good: Horrabin had indeed intended the position of the body to suggest murder. But might he not have left other less desirable indications? If he had, nothing could be done about it now, for here was the doctor and men with a stretcher.

'I'll ask you, doctor, not to move him for a few moments,' said Hubbard, and he explained about the photograph.

Dr Wheatley was taciturn and they waited practically in silence till the photographer came. Flashlight pictures were quickly taken and the remains were borne off. Hubbard turned to Horrabin.

'Thank you for your help, Mr Horrabin. I shall want a formal statement from you for my report, but tomorrow will be time enough. Doctor, if you've finished we might drive in together.'

Feeling himself dismissed, Horrabin returned to the hotel. There after an hour Vennor joined him. 'Mrs Perring asked me to run over to Lington to fetch her sister,' he explained. 'She's badly cut up about the thing, but at least she won't be alone.'

For some minutes they discussed the affair and then Vennor took himself off. Horrabin was fairly satisfied. He thought all had gone well and that he had only the raincoat in the cistern to worry about. This he could not remove at the moment, but he would take it in a parcel to London in a day or so and during the night drop it over one of the bridges into the Thames.

Next day Inspector Hubbard came to the office and took his statement. Horrabin explained that he was working on some reports all evening and knew nothing about the affair till Vennor called him. Hubbard seemed satisfied, thanked him politely, and withdrew. All was well.

The following evening when the hotel was quiet Horrabin took the first step to relieve himself of his dangerous evidence. He crept up to the tank room for the raincoat, which next day he would take to London. Silently he bared his arm and plunged it into the water. Yes, all still was well: there was the package as he had left it. He drew it gently up and held it to let the water drain away.

Then suddenly he had a feeling that he was not alone. He swung round. There watching him from the door was Inspector Hubbard. His heart seemed to stand still as he dropped the raincoat and slowly stood up. Dimly he saw Hubbard move forward and a second policeman appear at the door. Then the room went black and he felt himself falling into emptiness.

★   ★   ★

'Yes, sir, I got Horrabin easily enough,' Hubbard said later to his old chief, Superintendent French, whom he accidentally met in the train. 'From the very start it looked like murder. First, the deceased should have been over the crossing before the train was due. Then there was no injury from the bufferbeam where you'd expect it if he was standing up when hit, nor was the coat marked by the ballast, as it would if the body had been thrown forcibly down. The back of the head was practically torn off, and it seemed to me it must have been propped up against the rail. Not conclusive of course, but suspicious.'

'I'll say so,' French agreed.

'I took the obvious further step. If it was murder, who might be guilty? First I thought Vennor was my man. I saw what looked like blood on his raincoat and further examination showed rust and oily grit which might have come from the track. When I pointed these out to him he seemed completely taken aback and swore he could not explain them. I then asked him had he stooped over the body when he found it. Though he must have seen that this might account for the marks, he assured me he had not. This inclined me to look elsewhere before coming to a conclusion.

'I knew that he and Horrabin lived at the same hotel and that both were partners of the deceased. The trouble might have been connected with the business and if so, Horrabin was also worth considering. I had noticed also that he and Vennor were about the same size and either could have worn the coat.

'But from a timetable of the actions of both men I saw that I was wrong. Horrabin could not have worn the coat. If Vennor's statement was true, as I was assuming, it was hanging in his room at the time of the murder. Then I remembered that Vennor had been requested to make a bogus telephone call at ten. I asked myself why?

'Obviously to get Vennor out of the room. But again why? Suddenly the possibility of a duplicate raincoat occurred to me. His own could have been changed while he was at dinner, but something like the bogus call would have been necessary to get it replaced. What else indeed could the call have been for? And then: who but Horrabin could have worked the scheme?

'While Horrabin was at his office I searched for the coat. He could scarcely have taken it out of the hotel unobserved with the watch we had kept and I confined my efforts to the building. Soon I found it in the tank. Then I thought it might be a good idea to let the man convict himself, so I shadowed him and turned up in the tank room at the critical moment.'

'You both got your deserts,' French declared as the story ended: 'you your win and he his loss.'

FREEMAN WILLS CROFTS

THE BOX OFFICE MURDERS

A London box office clerk falls under the spell of a mysterious trio of crooks. Assisted by a helpful solicitor who directs her to Scotland Yard, she tells Inspector French the story of the Purple Sickle. But when her body is found floating in Southampton Water the next day, French discovers that similar murders have taken place and determines to learn the trio's secret and run them to ground...

THE HOG'S BACK MYSTERY

Several local residents have disappeared in suspicious circumstances at The Hog's Back ridge in Surrey. When a doctor vanishes, followed by a nurse with whom he was acquainted, Inspector French deduces murder, but there are no bodies. Can he eventually prove his theory and show that murder has been committed?

'As pretty a piece of work as Inspector French has done...on the level of Mr Crofts' very best; which is saying something.'

– E C Bentley in the *Daily Telegraph*

FREEMAN WILLS CROFTS

INSPECTOR FRENCH'S GREATEST CASE

A head clerk's corpse is discovered beside the empty safe of a Hatton Garden diamond merchant. There are many suspects and a multitude of false clues to be followed before a tireless investigator is called in to solve the crime. This is a case for Freeman Wills Crofts' most famous character – Inspector French.

MAN OVERBOARD!

In the course of a ship's passage from Belfast to Liverpool, a man disappears and his body is later picked up by Irish fishermen. Although the coroner's verdict is suicide, murder is suspected. Inspector French co-operates with Superintendent Rainey and Sergeant McClung once more to determine the truth, whatever the cost...

'To me, Inspector French is the most human sleuth
to be found in the detective novels of today.'
– *Punch*

FREEMAN WILLS CROFTS

MYSTERY IN THE CHANNEL

The cross-channel steamer *Chichester* stops halfway to France. A motionless yacht lies in her path and when a party clambers aboard it finds a trail of blood and two dead men. Chief Constable Turnbill has to call on the ever-reliable Inspector French for help in solving the mystery of the *Nymph*.

MYSTERY ON SOUTHAMPTON WATER

The Joymount Rapid Hardening Cement Manufacturing Company is in serious financial trouble. Two young company employees hatch a plot to break into a rival works on the Isle of Wight to find out their competitor's secret for undercutting them. But the scheme does not go according to plan and results in the death of a night watchman, theft and fire. Inspector French is brought in to solve the baffling mystery.

OTHER TITLES BY FREEMAN WILLS CROFTS AVAILABLE DIRECT
FROM HOUSE OF STRATUS

Quantity		£	$(US)	$(CAN)	€
	THE 12.30 FROM CROYDON	6.99	12.95	19.95	13.50
	THE AFFAIR AT LITTLE WOKEHAM	6.99	12.95	19.95	13.50
	ANTIDOTE TO VENOM	6.99	12.95	19.95	13.50
	ANYTHING TO DECLARE?	6.99	12.95	19.95	13.50
	THE BOX OFFICE MURDERS	6.99	12.95	19.95	13.50
	THE CASK	6.99	12.95	19.95	13.50
	CRIME AT GUILDFORD	6.99	12.95	19.95	13.50
	DEATH OF A TRAIN	6.99	12.95	19.95	13.50
	DEATH ON THE WAY	6.99	12.95	19.95	13.50
	THE END OF ANDREW HARRISON	6.99	12.95	19.95	13.50
	ENEMY UNSEEN	6.99	12.95	19.95	13.50
	FATAL VENTURE	6.99	12.95	19.95	13.50
	FEAR COMES TO CHALFONT	6.99	12.95	19.95	13.50
	FOUND FLOATING	6.99	12.95	19.95	13.50
	FRENCH STRIKES OIL	6.99	12.95	19.95	13.50
	GOLDEN ASHES	6.99	12.95	19.95	13.50
	THE GROOTE PARK MURDER	6.99	12.95	19.95	13.50
	THE HOG'S BACK MYSTERY	6.99	12.95	19.95	13.50
	INSPECTOR FRENCH AND THE CHEYNE MYSTERY	6.99	12.95	19.95	13.50

ALL HOUSE OF STRATUS BOOKS ARE AVAILABLE FROM GOOD BOOKSHOPS
OR DIRECT FROM THE PUBLISHER:

Internet: **www.houseofstratus.com** including synopses and features.

Email: **sales@houseofstratus.com**
info@houseofstratus.com
(please quote author, title and credit card details.)

OTHER TITLES BY FREEMAN WILLS CROFTS AVAILABLE DIRECT FROM HOUSE OF STRATUS

Quantity		£	$(US)	$(CAN)	€
☐	INSPECTOR FRENCH AND THE STARVEL TRAGEDY	6.99	12.95	19.95	13.50
☐	INSPECTOR FRENCH'S GREATEST CASE	6.99	12.95	19.95	13.50
☐	JAMES TARRANT, ADVENTURER	6.99	12.95	19.95	13.50
☐	A LOSING GAME	6.99	12.95	19.95	13.50
☐	THE LOSS OF THE JANE VOSPER	6.99	12.95	19.95	13.50
☐	MAN OVERBOARD!	6.99	12.95	19.95	13.50
☐	MANY A SLIP	6.99	12.95	19.95	13.50
☐	MURDERERS MAKE MISTAKES	6.99	12.95	19.95	13.50
☐	MYSTERY IN THE CHANNEL	6.99	12.95	19.95	13.50
☐	MYSTERY ON SOUTHAMPTON WATER	6.99	12.95	19.95	13.50
☐	THE PIT-PROP SYNDICATE	6.99	12.95	19.95	13.50
☐	THE PONSON CASE	6.99	12.95	19.95	13.50
☐	THE SEA MYSTERY	6.99	12.95	19.95	13.50
☐	SILENCE FOR THE MURDERER	6.99	12.95	19.95	13.50
☐	SIR JOHN MAGILL'S LAST JOURNEY	6.99	12.95	19.95	13.50
☐	SUDDEN DEATH	6.99	12.95	19.95	13.50

ALL HOUSE OF STRATUS BOOKS ARE AVAILABLE FROM GOOD BOOKSHOPS
OR DIRECT FROM THE PUBLISHER:

Tel: Order Line
          0800 169 1780 (UK)
          1 800 724 1100 (USA)
          International
          +44 (0) 1845 527700 (UK)
          +01   845 463 1100 (USA)

Fax: +44 (0) 1845 527711 (UK)
          +01   845 463 0018 (USA)
          (please quote author, title and credit card details.)

Send to: House of Stratus Sales Department   House of Stratus Inc.
          Thirsk Industrial Park   2 Neptune Road
          York Road, Thirsk   Poughkeepsie
          North Yorkshire, YO7 3BX   NY 12601
          UK   USA

PAYMENT

Please tick currency you wish to use:

☐ £ (Sterling)   ☐ $ (US)   ☐ $ (CAN)   ☐ € (Euros)

Allow for shipping costs charged per order plus an amount per book as set out in the tables below:

CURRENCY/DESTINATION

	£(Sterling)	$(US)	$(CAN)	€(Euros)
Cost per order				
UK	1.50	2.25	3.50	2.50
Europe	3.00	4.50	6.75	5.00
North America	3.00	3.50	5.25	5.00
Rest of World	3.00	4.50	6.75	5.00
Additional cost per book				
UK	0.50	0.75	1.15	0.85
Europe	1.00	1.50	2.25	1.70
North America	1.00	1.00	1.50	1.70
Rest of World	1.50	2.25	3.50	3.00

PLEASE SEND CHEQUE OR INTERNATIONAL MONEY ORDER
payable to: HOUSE OF STRATUS LTD or HOUSE OF STRATUS INC. or card payment as indicated

STERLING EXAMPLE

Cost of book(s):......................Example: 3 x books at £6.99 each: £20.97
Cost of order:.......................Example: £1.50 (Delivery to UK address)
Additional cost per book:...............Example: 3 x £0.50: £1.50
Order total including shipping:...........Example: £23.97

VISA, MASTERCARD, SWITCH, AMEX:

☐ ☐ ☐ ☐ ☐ ☐ ☐ ☐ ☐ ☐ ☐ ☐ ☐ ☐ ☐ ☐ ☐ ☐ ☐ ☐

Issue number (Switch only):

☐ ☐ ☐

Start Date: Expiry Date:

☐ ☐ / ☐ ☐   ☐ ☐ / ☐ ☐

Signature: _____

NAME: _____

ADDRESS: _____

COUNTRY: _____

ZIP/POSTCODE: _____

Please allow 28 days for delivery. Despatch normally within 48 hours.

Prices subject to change without notice.
Please tick box if you do not wish to receive any additional information. ☐

House of Stratus publishes many other titles in this genre; please check our website (**www.houseofstratus.com**) for more details.